TEEN FLL

P9-DMX-058

The greats.

PRICE: $20.00 (3798/tfarp)

THE GREATS

The Greats

Deborah Ellis

Groundwood Books
House of Anansi Press
Toronto / Berkeley

Groundwood Books / House of Anansi Press
groundwoodbooks.com

We gratefully acknowledge for their financial support of our publishing program the Canada Council for the Arts, the Ontario Arts Council and the Government of Canada.

 Canada Council for the Arts · Conseil des Arts du Canada

 ONTARIO ARTS COUNCIL
CONSEIL DES ARTS DE L'ONTARIO
an Ontario government agency
un organisme du gouvernement de l'Ontario

With the participation of the Government of Canada
Avec la participation du gouvernement du Canada |  Canada

Library and Archives Canada Cataloguing in Publication
Title: The greats / Deborah Ellis.
Names: Ellis, Deborah, author.
Identifiers: Canadiana (print) 20190228091 | Canadiana (ebook) 20190228105 | ISBN 9781773063874 (hardcover) | ISBN 9781773063881 (EPUB) | ISBN 9781773063898 (Kindle)
Classification: LCC PS8559.L5494 G74 2020 | DDC jC813/.54—dc23

Jacket design by Michael Solomon
Jacket illustration by Byron Eggenschwiler

Groundwood Books is committed to protecting our natural environment. This book is made of material from well-managed FSC®-certified forests, recycled materials, and other controlled sources.

Printed and bound in Canada

FSC MIX Paper from responsible sources FSC® C016245
www.fsc.org

All royalties from the sale of this book will be donated to Mental Health Without Borders. mhwb.ca

1

There is a leak in the wall of Guyana's national museum.

Rain drools down the plaster. The leak gets bigger with each downpour. It threatens to damage the museum's most expensive exhibit.

In a large room on the ground floor is a giant prehistoric ground sloth, standing on her haunches, arms reaching up into an artificial cannonball tree.

Megatherium. Gather to her friends and to the people who come to see her.

The officials don't think the leak is a big problem, so they ignore it.

The leak gets bigger.

The officials decide to put a patch over it.

Covering up a problem only makes it worse. The heavy Guyana rainwater pools inside the wall, then spreads out to become many leaks.

Water snakes across the floor, putting the treasured exhibit in peril.

By the time the officials decide to do the work necessary to fix what is really wrong, the damaged wall has to be completely taken down, and a new, stronger wall needs to be built in its place.

It takes the workers a whole day to take down the wall. At the end of the day, they hang big sheets of plastic over the gap, secure the sheets with bricks and boards, then head home to their families.

The sky is dark. The museum is quiet.

The only movement is the night breeze, tickling the edges of the plastic, looking for a way inside.

2

Friday night, and Jomon is alone at the party.

He is sitting at a crowded table in a crowded banquet room at a Chinese restaurant in Georgetown, just down the street from the national museum. The lights are bright, the voices are loud, and the first-place medal is heavy around his neck.

Jomon's body is in the chair, but his mind is far, far away.

"Off in Jomonland," his mother used to call it when he got lost in his head. She named the place when he was eight years old and she was tired of fighting for his attention.

"You're just like your father," she said — one of the few times she said it with a smile. "If you're going to

11

disappear like he does, let's at least make sure you have a good place to go."

Mum sat him down at the kitchen table and brought out the crayons. She sat beside him and said, "Draw someplace beautiful."

He drew a clearing in the forest. Tree branches came together overhead like the roof of the cathedral. He drew green grass, cool and soft. He put a brook along one side, gurgling and bubbling. He didn't draw birds — not that time — but he knew they were there, singing to each other, enjoying the day, expecting nothing from him.

"You need a place to sit," Mum said.

With a brown crayon, Jomon drew a straight-backed chair, the only chair he knew how to draw.

Mum gently took the crayon from him. She extended the lines of the chair and turned it into a bench.

"You might sometimes want me in Jomonland with you," she said.

But tonight, drought has come to Jomonland. Everything is gray. The bench is broken, his mum is dead, and he is stuck all alone at this stupid party.

He should have gone straight home after the final competition, but he thought the dinner might salvage the night.

It hasn't.

Months of study, practices, regional competitions

and frayed nerves all came to an end barely two hours ago with Jomon and the rest of Team Durban Park winning the Guyanese National High School Geography Competition. All four students received medals. If they were lucky enough to be accepted to the University of Guyana (which for Jomon, the team's youngest, was still over three years away), they would get scholarships to cover some of their tuition.

Jomon knows he should feel thrilled.

All he feels is empty.

Again.

What now?

Jomon shoves the remains of a spring roll into his mouth to chase the question away, but the question refuses to go.

What is there now?

The banquet room is full of students, teachers and community members. Geography teams from all over Guyana are eating, laughing and talking over every minute of the weeks-long competition, from school-wide to city-wide, from regionals to nationals. Teachers and politicians give speeches, congratulating the students and congratulating themselves.

Bits of conversation swirl around Jomon.

"Remember when I said Tropic of Copernicus instead of Tropic of Capricorn?"

"After tonight, I never have to think about who controls the Nicobar Islands. Unless I want to go there — and I might!"

On and on it goes.

The bright lights bounce off the three other gold medals in the room. Jomon's teammates. While the competition was going on, Jomon could pretend they were mates — a team, all for one and one for all. But the competition is over. Jomon sees it for the lie that it is. The three other Team Durban Park members are scattered around the room, probably happy to be rid of him, enjoying the company of their friends and family.

Jomon has no family at the party.

As far as he is concerned, he has no family at all.

Other kids' parents pat him on the back and say "Congratulations!" on their way to talk to who they really want to talk to. "You're a young man with a terrific future ahead of you!"

Terrific future? Who were they kidding? He knew he'd never get to Terrific.

He could pretend otherwise, for a time. The competition kept him busy with hours of studying at the library and at home, filling his head with the prime meridian, medieval cartographers, inland seas and Asian mountain ranges. Geography kept him going.

Now it's done. The heaviness is back. The gray ghost

that lives behind his eyes has room again to take over, blocking out colors, turning everything sour.

Jomon watches the other people in the room. They talk easy. They laugh easy. They pose for pictures.

I am a different species, he thinks. *I don't belong here. I don't belong anywhere.*

The party is torture and he can't stand it one more second. He gets to his feet.

"You're not leaving?"

A man who is a candidate in the upcoming election and one of the sponsors of the competition, gently pushes Jomon back into his chair.

"The party is just getting started. Look, they're bringing out more food!" the man says. "Let's get that plate filled up! All that studying has made you too skinny. The ladies like some meat on the bones. Eat up. There's room on my campaign for a bright young man. Of course, it doesn't pay in money, but experience! That's the real thing. Your teacher tells me you also ran a charity book drive. Now you can go back to all those people and ask them to vote for me."

Jomon thinks about saying that the book drive is an assignment for social studies class, that all the students have to do a community project, that he did it with four other students and he didn't even take the lead.

But he doesn't bother. It doesn't matter.

The candidate keeps talking as he loads up Jomon's plate with food. Jomon eats. He can taste that the food is good, but it gives him no pleasure. When the candidate moves on to someone else, Jomon puts down his fork.

How are things in Jomonland? he can almost hear his mother ask.

Bad, Mum. Real bad.

How can he be at a celebration, surrounded by nice people who say good things about him, and all he wants to do is disappear?

"What's wrong with me?" he whispers to his plate.

The celebration crawls along. The *Chronicle* shows up, and Jomon has to pose for pictures with his team, smile on his face, medal held up beside his cheek.

"This will be online in an hour," the reporter says, "and you can see it in print in tomorrow's edition."

It's easy after that to step away from the group. No one calls after him. He walks out of the banquet room, down the stairs, out of the restaurant and onto the street.

The darkness is a relief.

Jomon takes the medal from around his neck and shoves it in his trouser pocket. He walks slowly through the streets, past people in church clothes heading home from evening prayer meetings, past couples heading out to the bars, and tourists finding their way back to their hotels. He moves through it all as if he is invisible.

Exams are coming up. Okay. He'll study hard for them. That should keep him going until the end of the school year. He'll get a job during the break, delivering groceries, doing odd jobs, whatever he can find. He'll be away from home all day. He'll save his pay in a bank account where his father can't get at it.

Good. This is a good plan. Hard work, long hours, earning money and keeping it safe. He'll be too tired at the end of each day to feel any damn feelings or ask any damn questions.

Then school will start up again. He'll try out for the geography team again. Maybe they'll win first place again and eat more Chinese food at the celebration.

And afterwards, he'll walk home slowly through the dark Georgetown night, looking for a reason to keep living.

He just feels so tired.

Jomon turns into his block. Maybe he should have told his father about the event tonight. Dad has been drinking less lately. Even made dinner one night, that spicy chicken dish of Mum's. Jomon walked into the house, took one sniff of the familiar aroma and walked out again.

Maybe he shouldn't have done that. Maybe he should give his father a chance. Maybe nine months of silence is enough to punish him.

Jomon's hands curl into fists.

Nine months isn't enough. Always and forever would not be enough.

The house is dark when he gets home. Of course it is. His father drank the electric bill money. Probably drank the rent money, too.

Jomon kicks at a beer can on his way to his small bedroom. His father is out at the bar. Just another Friday night.

Jomon shuts the door of his room, pushes off his shoes and falls onto the bed fully dressed in his school uniform. He feels so miserable that he sings to himself the song his father used to sing to him when he was little. Dad calls it the Soothing Song.

Chatter monkeys in the trees
Swaying branches in the breeze
Sleep the hours of dark away
Wake up to a brighter day.

He finally drops into sleep. He dreams of food platters multiplying around him, stacking up like prison walls, giving him no way out.

3

While Jomon is sleeping, Gather is waking up.

The night breeze, fresh from the Caribbean Sea, slips into the exhibit hall through the gaps in the plastic sheeting. It inches around, exploring, discovering new territory, taking up new space.

It winds its way around Gather's tree-trunk legs, then swirls over her strong belly and shoulders. It breathes a thousand scents into her nostrils. A thousand tastes dance on her tongue.

It whispers in her ears, "Come out!"

Gather smells and tastes and hears.

And wakes up.

She moves her arm, just a little. It is stiff from being posed in one spot for such a long time. She moves it some more. She wiggles her long claws. She sways her ˙

hips. Then she puts one foot out in front of her. She moves her other foot.

Soon she is at the plastic wall.

She pushes it aside as if it is fog.

Gather is quiet. She makes not a sound as she slips out onto the street.

She fills her lungs.

It is good to be alive.

Again.

4

Now Jomon is running. In his stocking feet.

It is three o'clock in the morning.

He doesn't remember waking up. He doesn't remember leaving his house or why he is running. He doesn't remember the loud *SLAM* of the door hitting the wall as he bombed through and he doesn't remember the second *SLAM* as the door banged shut into place behind him, or the light of the neighbor lady, awakened by the noise.

He doesn't remember his feet slipping on the steps from his porch and sending him tumbling to the cement landing. Later he'll notice the bruises but he won't wonder about them. He's used to bruises. For his father, drinking and hitting go together.

Jomon keeps running down the middle of the street until a cabbie honks him out of the way. Then he runs along the side of the street, in the gravel and up on the sidewalks, jumping on and off curbs.

Running, running, running.

Jomon puts his foot down where there should be cement but instead there is a hole in the sidewalk. His whole leg plunges into the water flowing in a gutter below. His face hits the pavement nose first and his other leg bends beneath him.

Blood gushes.

Jomon pulls his foot out of the water, wipes the blood from his face with his shirt sleeve and starts running again. He runs with a bit of a limp, but he does not let that slow him down.

He keeps running lopsidedly until he reaches the liquor store.

Jomon pants heavily as he glares at that store. He grabs the closest thing he can reach, a handful of pebbles, and pelts them at the window.

The gravel just tinkles like fairy dust against the bars and the glass.

He runs up to the store and kicks it, hurting his foot and making him madder. He grabs the window bars and tries to shake them apart. He looks around for a proper tool to use against the hateful building, but the street is too clean. There is nothing he can use.

Then he remembers.

He does have something.

In his pocket is the geography medal. He takes it out. Its gleam mocks him.

All that work, and your life is the same! All that work, and YOU are the same! You are nothing! You will always be nothing!

Jomon begins the wind-up, like David preparing to slay Goliath with his slingshot.

David knew his slingshot would send the stone right into the giant's head. Jomon knows his medal will fly strong right through the pane of glass.

Jomon lets the medal soar and watches it go. The medal crashes right through the window. Shards of glass sparkle like stars in the streetlight.

The flying medal makes a big hole in the window. Jomon needs to make it bigger. He runs to the store, and with his fist he punches in as much of the window as he can reach, smash after smash, not stopping until the window pane is as clear as he can make it, the broken glass tinkling against the bottles of rum and gin inside.

Jomon stops then and catches his breath. He holds up his hands and sees the blood running from them.

But he's still angry.

He starts running again.

He doesn't get far.

A police car drives right up in front of Jomon, and when he turns to go in another direction, another police car blocks his way.

Foolishly, he tries to fight his way through the police officers, but there are too many and they are older, bigger and stronger. He is slammed belly down against a car. His arms are yanked back, and cuffs are twisted around his wrists.

Still he tries to get away.

"Stop fighting us," a woman's voice says loudly next to his ear. "We've got you now. There is nowhere for you to go except with us. So take a deep breath and quit fighting."

Jomon does not want to take a deep breath, but the police keep him pinned down on the hood of the car, waiting for him to give in. He keeps them waiting.

His face is pressed against the car, right cheek down. Through the arms of the officers, he can see the empty street.

Out of the corner of his eye, he thinks he sees something move. It looks bigger than a house, but whatever it is moves in shadows, and Jomon can't see it clearly.

Jomon is distracted and stops fighting long enough for the police officers to stop leaning on him. He feels the officers ease off and he starts fighting them again.

He fights with his feet as they shove him in the back of the car. He fights the car seat with his head as they drive him to the police station. He fights and fights, and by the time they arrive at the police station, he has no fight left.

All he has is pain.

5

"Sit."

Jomon relents to the pressure the officer puts on his shoulder and sits in the chair beside her desk. He rubs his wrists, glad that the handcuffs have been taken off.

The officer sits down at her computer.

"Let's start with your name," she says. Then, before he can make it clear he isn't going to answer her, she asks, "Where are your shoes?"

Jomon looks at his wet, bloody feet in his wet, bloody socks, then tucks them under his chair. They leave a smear of blood and water on the light-gray police-station floor.

"Looks like you stepped in some glass," the officer said. "And were you in a fight? There's blood on your face, too, and on your shirt and hands. That's a school uniform you're wearing, isn't it? Why are you wearing your uniform at this hour?"

She does not wait for him to answer. She gets up and walks away.

Jomon looks at her desktop. A name plate reads *Officer Olivia Grant*. A notepad, a pen, a telephone, and a computer are neatly arranged. On a corner of the desk sits a small photo in a frame made out of painted ice-cream sticks. In the photo, two youngsters in yellow-and-white school uniforms beam at the camera.

The youngsters are a boy and a girl. They look about the same age. Jomon wonders if they're twins. He guesses their bellies are full. Kids don't smile like that when their bellies are empty.

Officer Grant returns with a basin of water. She has a towel and first-aid kit tucked under her arm. She puts the basin on the floor, the kit and the towel on her desk, and sits down.

"Give me your feet," she orders.

It is such an unexpected command that Jomon obeys before realizing he doesn't want to. Officer Grant peels off his filthy socks and sticks his feet in the warm water of the basin. She takes a bottle of Dettol out of the kit and adds a capful to the water. The steam takes on an antiseptic smell. It is soothing.

Jomon is no fool. He does not want infected feet. The warm water feels good.

"Thank you," he whispers.

"You're welcome," says Officer Grant. "Are you ready to tell me your name? Age? Address? Why were you breaking windows and running the streets in the dark hours of the morning?"

Jomon shakes his head.

"Your parents are going to be worried." She slides the notepad and pen closer to him. "Write down their phone number. Write an address. They have the right to know you are safe."

Jomon's lips curl into a sneer. It is a slight sneer. Jomon is not a sneering sort of boy, so his sneer is a reaction rather than an attitude.

Officer Grant sees it. She frowns and nods and leaves him alone again.

Jomon feels like a fool sitting in the police station with his feet in a basin. He looks around the room to see if anyone is laughing at him.

Men and women in uniforms sit at desks, talk on phones, sip coffee and look at their computers. No one seems to be paying attention to him.

Two officers bring in a prisoner, a man they half walk, half drag into the room.

"It was a cat," the man slurs. "It was a giant cat. No, a rat! A rat, as big as a house!"

"Is it a full moon?" the desk sergeant asks. "I've had two calls tonight about giant animals."

"Cats or rats?" one of the arresting officers asks, as he keeps moving the drunken man through to a chair beside a desk.

"Clean your face with this." Officer Grant reappears at Jomon's side and hands him a wet cloth.

Jomon wipes his face, scrubbing at the blood that has dried on his cheeks.

"Now I can see you," Officer Grant says. "You're not a bad-looking kid. You take after your father or your mother? What is their phone number, by the way? Will you write it down for me so I can call them? Will you write down your address?"

Jomon does not answer.

"Are you able to write?" Officer Grant asks quietly. "No shame if you can't. That happens sometimes. Can you read and write?"

Jomon nods.

"You are saying you can write the address but you are choosing not to. Is that correct?

Jomon nods again.

"All right," she says. "We're getting somewhere." She takes another damp cloth and wipes the dried blood off his hands, examining the small cuts. She gives them a quick swab with Dettol and leaves them unbandaged. "Right foot, please."

Jomon thinks about refusing, but he has the strong suspicion that Officer Grant would have no problem letting him sit with his feet in the basin for an infinite amount of time. He will have to comply at some point. Better to do it now and get it over with.

Officer Grant spreads a towel over her knees to keep her uniform clean and dry. She dries off his foot, then inspects the cuts before applying first aid. All the while, she keeps talking. Her voice is low, casual, like a good teacher discussing how to tackle an algebra equation.

"I'm wondering now if you are afraid to tell me how to contact your parents because they will beat you. Maybe your father will hit you, maybe your mother, maybe both. I see some old bruises on your arms and face. Who's been hitting you, son?"

He doesn't reply.

She looks at Jomon's foot with a magnifying glass and uses tweezers to remove small bits of glass. She puts some antiseptic lotion on the cuts that makes his foot sting. He flinches.

"That hurts, doesn't it?" she says, wincing. "Some things have to hurt a bit before they get better. The lotion I put on your cuts will help them heal but first it will make them feel worse. It's like whatever is going on with you. Right now you think that by holding your tongue you will avoid pain. In the short term, you may be right. But the pain will only get bigger the longer you avoid it. Tell your story now, feel the pain, get it over with and move on. Destruction of property, attempted robbery of the liquor store, resisting arrest, assaulting a police officer. These are serious charges you are facing, but not so serious that you can't get through them and put them behind you. Especially since you are only thirteen."

"Fifteen," says Jomon.

"Fifteen," she says simply.

She stops talking then, finishing one foot and moving on to the other. This one also has bits of glass in it. She bandages him up, then takes the basin and the first-aid kit away.

Jomon squirms in his seat. The foot bath and the first aid have been humiliating, but even though the deepest cuts are throbbing, his feet feel better with the glass out and the antiseptic on.

"Gimme a smoke!" a man yells.

Jomon swivels around to see the drunk guy the police brought in handcuffed to a chair a few desks away from him.

"I want a smoke!" the man yells again. Then, like a balloon with a hole, all the energy drains out of him and he slumps back in his chair, face to the ceiling, snoring away.

Jomon watches him for a moment. A waft of booze reaches his nostrils. Jomon is afraid he is going to be sick. He covers his nose and turns away.

Officer Grant returns. A young police officer comes up to her desk with a clear plastic evidence bag in his hand. Jomon catches a glimpse of what is inside it.

"The owner of the liquor store says nothing was taken and no damage was done except for the broken window," the officer says. "She's going to have a lot of glass to clean up. She found this on the floor. Says it doesn't belong in her store."

"Thank you," says Officer Grant. The young cop leaves. Officer Grant takes the medal out of the bag and looks closely at it.

"2020 Guyanese National High School Geography Competition, First Place Team," she reads out loud. "Is this yours?"

Jomon lowers his eyes. She turns to her computer, types a moment, then sits back and looks at the screen.

"Here it is," she says. "On the *Chronicle*'s website." She leans in to look at the photo and the caption. "Your name is Jomon Fowler and you are fifteen years old. You are a ninth-grade student at Durban Park Community High School. Let's see if I can access the school records. Yup, here they are. Your file says your mother is deceased and you live with your father on Hadfield Street near Durban Park. There's even a phone number here. Shall I call your father?"

Jomon can feel his body ache to run, to flip over the

desk and jump through a window. No more questions! He wants out!

"Shall I call your father?" Officer Grant repeats.

Jomon stands up. He has to get out of that police station and away from this nosy Officer Grant.

"I need you to sit," Officer Grant says, standing beside him and putting her hands on his shoulders. "If you are not safe at home, we can protect you, but sit down and together we will telephone your father."

Jomon spins away so that all Officer Grant has is a grip on one arm. He tries to pull away but she will not let him loose.

"Jomon, calm down," Officer Grant says. "Remember where you are. You cannot behave like this in here. Sit down now and I will call your father."

Jomon snaps. He yells right in her face. "Call my father? Go ahead! Call him! Call him!"

He is a trapped animal. His chest heaves with air he cannot get in or out.

And then he throws up. Vomit shoots out from his throat and onto the police-station floor.

He is hauled through the station and into the lockup. Cell doors bang as adult prisoners are moved to accommodate him.

"Juvenile," Officer Grant says. "Extra protection and extra consideration."

She cuts through the grumbling from the prisoners.

"Come on, gentlemen. Would you want your young son in the same cell with a bunch of grown men? Get a move on and consider it your good deed for the day."

His school tie is taken off him. Then he is pushed into the cell. With his last bit of fight, he throws himself from wall to wall. Officer Grant stands at the bars and watches him.

"There's no need for that," she says quietly. "Calm yourself. You are a competition winner, so I know you know how to control your nerves. Employ those skills now. Don't make things worse for yourself."

She leaves him in the lockup. The door bangs shut.

The cell block fills with the jeers and shouts of the other prisoners. They're mad at being moved, mad at being crowded in together.

Jomon sits on the metal slab bed and puts his head in his hands. He tries to summon the old Jomonland, the green trees and the cool grass. He used to be able to do it when his father was raging, but he can't do it now. The angry voices and the putrid smells of vomit, disinfectant, missed toilets and fear are keeping him too rooted in the real. It's all he can do to keep breathing.

"Hey, little baby!" prisoners call out to him. They make noises of babies crying. They say rude things. They threaten him with beatings and worse. Jomon keeps his face in his hands and doesn't respond.

Eventually, they leave him alone and complain to each other.

Jomon raises his head to look at where he's landed.

The cell has three sides made of cinder blocks, one with a tiny, grimy window too high up to see out. The fourth wall of the cell is made of bars, including a barred door.

Jomon looks across the hallway to the cell facing him. It's empty. He's glad there's no one there to watch and bother him.

Jomon curls into the least uncomfortable position he can manage on the hard bed. There is no pillow to cushion his head and no blanket to pull up over his face. He breathes in foulness. He keeps his eyes open, staring at the tiny window, willing the daylight to come but not having any hope that dawn will make anything better.

Officer Grant comes to see him at the end of her shift. She talks to him through the cell bars.

"You'll be in here until court on Monday," she says. "Don't lie to the judge and don't refuse to talk. If you want to be released, you'll have to have a responsible adult in the courtroom to take control of you, either a parent or officially designated guardian. Do you understand?"

Jomon remains curled up and doesn't respond.

"Sit up when I'm talking to you!"

Officer Grant's tone sounds so much like his mother's

when she was having no nonsense that Jomon automatically sits up.

"Look at me," orders Officer Grant.

He looks at her.

"Do you understand what you need to do if you want to be released?"

Jomon nods.

"Ask one of the officers to make a phone call for you," Officer Grant says. "I've tried to phone your father, but the number is out of service. I drove to the address on your school records, but your family was evicted almost a year ago. You shouldn't be going through this alone, but I can't help you unless you talk to me. You've got some serious charges. It's bad but it's not the end of the world. You can still get through this and put it behind you. Is there anything you want to tell me before I go?"

Jomon shakes his head. He doesn't want her to leave him alone in this place, but he doesn't say so. He figures there's no point.

"All right, then," says Officer Grant. "I'm going home to cook breakfast for my kids. You behave. You can make this better for yourself or you can make it a whole lot worse."

With that, she leaves.

Jomon rushes to the bars and presses his face against

them. He has to bite his tongue to keep from calling her back.

He doesn't have anything to say to her.

He just doesn't want to be left alone.

Alone with his thoughts.

And nothing else.

6

As Jomon faces his first morning behind bars, Mrs. Simson arrives at the national museum to begin her day.

As usual, she is the first to arrive. Cleaners generally are. The bosses don't want to deal with dust and garbage, not even to see it being removed. Cleaners come to a jobsite very early or very late and have the place to themselves.

Mrs. Simson, a widow, started cleaning at the museum back when she was still in high school. She wanted to earn money to go to university to study anthropology, but while she was sweeping the floors she got swept off her feet by a man with more charm than sense. All her earnings went into cleaning up his messes and paying down his debts, even after he died in a car accident.

She was sad and bitter for a time, but she's made her peace with it. She got her education at the public library, which is right next to the museum, and she thinks about what she's learned while she cleans the exhibits.

Mrs. Simson is an efficient cleaner, wiping fingerprints off the glass cases containing the taxidermied capybaras, caimans and birds and running her mop from room to room, gallery to gallery, from insect displays to collections of early gold-mining tools.

At the very end of her route is Gather's room.

She isn't planning to clean in here because she knows the wall is being repaired, but she always likes to say hello to Gather. She knows it's silly, but it feels like she and Gather are friends. There aren't many people in her life that she can talk to. There are the other people who work at the museum, but they generally don't talk to her, except to tell her that some visitor has spilled coffee or tracked in muddy footprints. There are people at church, and they're friendly, but she doesn't see them outside of services. There are people at the library, but they, too, have their noses in books. They are there to read and learn, not to have conversations.

But Gather is always here, always ready to listen.

Mrs. Simson tells Gather everything, good and bad, big and small. She tells Gather what groceries she needs to buy after work, about the stray cat she feeds who lets her get a teeny bit closer every day, about a beautiful sunrise and about being scared that she'll die alone. When Mrs. Simson can't sleep, she imagines Gather's gigantic arms wrapped around her, Gather's claws acting like armor, keeping her safe.

Mrs. Simson would feel more foolish about telling her life to Gather if she hadn't heard so many other people tell their troubles to the giant sloth over the years. As a cleaner, she is invisible. She can be standing right close to someone, wiping and polishing, but they don't notice her. They whisper to Gather: "The cancer is back. How will I tell my children?" "If I fail this test, my parents will hate me." "I like this girl at school, but she likes someone else." "I hate my boss. I should be running that place, not him!"

The giant ground sloth takes everything in and passes it on to no one. She knows how to keep secrets.

Mrs. Simson goes down the stairs and through the door into Gather's exhibit hall. Dawn is on the other side of the protective plastic and the room is soft with calm gray light.

Mrs. Simson has already read everything about Gather. The Megatherium's bones were discovered by miners in Omai and Oko Creek, down by the Cuyuni River. The discovery put Guyana on the paleontology map. Artists and curators took great care to recreate Gather in a setting that would be natural for her, with paintings and fake trees and shrubs. The exhibit was a huge achievement. Gather got her name in a nation-wide Name the Sloth competition. Guyana is very proud of her.

Mrs. Simson walks over to the bench facing the exhibit and sits down. She looks up …

At nothing.

She blinks, not quite believing what she is not seeing. Then she foolishly does what anyone would do. She looks under the bench, behind the fake trees, and even opens the secret door into the supply closet. She knows full well that not even Gather's paw would fit into any of these places.

Mrs. Simson's heart is beating so loud that she almost misses the soft rustle of the loosened plastic in the gentle morning breeze.

She tiptoes to the plastic. There, on the floor, in the dust the workers have left behind, are two footprints — massive, extinct, ground sloth footprints.

Gather has gone for a walk.

7

Jomon is trapped inside his nightmare.

He has *nothing* to do.

No books, no television, no homework, no distractions. He has no way to keep track of the passage of time. He has no way out and no way to get away from the *what now* question that comes at him like a tidal wave, screaming at him, drowning him. If his feet weren't bandaged, if he had shoes, maybe he could jump high enough to see out the window, if the window wasn't so grimy.

But his feet are sore and he doesn't want the bandages to come off, in case they don't give him new ones.

WHAT IS THERE NOW?

He tries to sleep. He can't.

He pictures Officer Grant going home to her kids and cooking them breakfast. He imagines their sleepy faces, their chirpy voices. It all makes him feel more alone.

As bad as his life was before, it's worse now. Before, he had his routine and the possibility that things might get better, that he would outrun the emptiness chasing him.

He misses the *what now* of yesterday. Yesterday, he could sometimes come up with an answer, like work hard at school, earn some money and hide it from Dad. Today, there is no point even trying.

He suffers through every long Saturday minute. Some prisoners sober up and leave and new ones come in. Jomon eats the meals of rice and peas, chewing without tasting. He smells the Dettol-soaked mops that are swirled back and forth between the cells.

Prisoners call out to him all day long — some friendly, some nosy, some disgusting, some mean. Jomon doesn't say a word.

Inside his head, the emptiness shows him his future.

There is sure to be something in the news about the broken window at the liquor store. Would they give his name?

Jomon can't remember if the names of teen criminals are printed in the paper or not. He's never paid attention to that before, since teen criminals had nothing to do with him. If his name isn't printed, they would print that a first-place geography medal was found at the scene. People would easily figure out who it belonged to. His school, his teammates, even that annoying politician who wanted him to work for free would know. They would say, "Oh, that rotten Jomon, shame on us for putting our faith in such a nothing boy."

He attends a public high school, so they will have to take him back when he gets out of jail — if he gets out — but they won't want him representing the school again. Without scholarship money he'll never be able to afford to go to university, and even if he could get work to pay for his tuition, would the university let in a criminal?

The daylight outside the small window gives way to dusk. The bright lights come on in the ceiling of the hallway. Jomon faces another night in lockup, then another day, then another night, and then court, where no one will stand with him to bail him out and take him home. More jail time will follow, and when he gets out, what?

The future that seemed hopeless yesterday seems glorious compared with what he pictures now.

Instead of graduating with a college degree, then getting a decent job in an office with a clean shirt and a good salary, he'll have to work much harder for less money. That's if anyone will hire him with a criminal record. And who would want him as a boyfriend — or a husband? No one, and why would they? He'll be all alone with a lousy job, bitter about life, probably drinking, probably hitting any woman who tries to come near him, just like his father hit his mother.

Why put himself and the world through that? The least he could do would be to spare others from having to deal with him.

Jomon's grandfather killed himself. His father often brought that up when he was drinking.

"The old man offed himself," Jomon can hear his father saying, with slurred words and boozy spit. "He didn't love me. And you don't love me. I'm going to do what my old man did. You wait."

And Jomon would say, "No, I love you, Mum loves you. Don't do it!"

Jomon used to say that. He hasn't said it in a while. He hasn't said anything to his father in a while.

Jomon feels a flutter of hope in his chest. Maybe there is a way out of all this after all.

If it's good enough for my grandfather.

He looks around the cell.

There is a place where the bars in the door meet the bars in the wall — a crossbar, a place to tie something.

He looks down at his school uniform shirt ...

"It won't be that easy," says a voice.

Jomon is startled. He looks in the direction of the voice.

It's coming from a boy around his age sitting in the cell across from him.

Jomon thinks he must have fallen asleep without realizing it. He doesn't remember the police bringing the other boy in.

"It's not that easy to hang yourself," the boy says again. "You get the knot wrong, you'll fall. You fall the wrong way, you break your spine and then you're alive but can't move. And even if you do it right, which is unlikely, it takes a long time to die by hanging. A long, painful time."

Jomon turns his back on the boy.

"Just because you can't see me doesn't mean I'm not here," says the boy. "And just because your mind thinks you want to die, don't count on your body agreeing. Your body will fight to stay alive. So, even if you get the knot right — which, again, is unlikely — you'll be up there fighting with yourself, getting your neck scarred up, probably pooping your pants, and at the end of it all, you'll be on the floor with a messed-up neck and poopy trousers. How does that make anything better?"

"Shut up," Jomon says, still with his back to the boy.

"I won't shut up. I'm telling you things you need to know. Although it doesn't really matter anyway because you take one step toward what you are thinking about doing, and I'll raise such a stink that every cop for miles around will come running to save you. Look at me when I'm talking to you! Give me some respect."

Jomon whips his head around.

"Why the hell should I respect you?"

The boy in the other cell just smiles and answers calmly.

"Because I am your great-great-grandfather. That's why."

8

Jomon's day is going from bad to worse.

"Shut up," he says again to the boy.

"Oh, very clever," the boy says.

There is no point trying to kill himself while that kid is watching him. Jomon has no doubt the boy will do as he says and stir up such a ruckus that the lockup will be flooded with officers in a second. But that kid won't be across from him forever. Jomon will wait and watch for his opportunity.

Jomon moves to the very back of his cell to try to get away from the annoying voice, but that only buys him another two feet of distance.

"I *am* your great-great-grandfather," the boy says again. "My name is Hiram Jomon Fowler. Folks call me Hi. You've heard of me."

Jomon has not but he doesn't say so. He doesn't want to do anything that might encourage Hi to keep talking.

But Hi needs no encouragement.

"Yes, you have," he says. "You're my great-great-grandson! I'm here to tell you there's been enough hanging in Guyana."

Jomon doesn't respond. That doesn't stop Hi.

"You don't agree? Hello, everybody!" Hi yells out to the rest of the cells. "Who here thinks there's been enough hanging in Guyana?"

The other residents shout back. "Too much hanging!" "Hanging's what the slave owners did to try to control us!" and "Shake my family tree, there's someone hanging from it. Shake all our family trees, same thing."

"See?" says Hi. "You don't know your family history, but you went to school. Must have studied something. Must have studied the slave uprisings in the 1700s, in the 1800s. They strung up bodies all over Georgetown and left them there to rot, while the white people danced in the streets."

Still Jomon says nothing.

"You have bad manners," says Hi. "Are you sure you're my great-great-grandson? Too much hanging. And you want to add another one. What's wrong with you?"

"Why are we talking about hanging?" says a voice from a cell down the hall.

"My great-great-grandson here is thinking of hanging himself," says Hi.

A heavy silence drops over the lockup.

"The boy is thinking of hanging himself?" one of the men asks in a quiet voice. "That young boy?"

"He is," says Hi.

"Don't do it," says the man.

"How old is he?" asks another man.

"He's fifteen," Hi tells him.

"Fifteen," the man repeats. "You got no trouble at fifteen."

Shut up, thinks Jomon. *What do you know about anything?*

"He thinks he's got nothing to live for," says Hi. "He thought he had nothing before he broke the law, but now that he's a criminal, he really thinks he's got nothing."

"That must mean he thinks we should all hang ourselves, too," another man says. "I don't like that, son, I don't like that at all. Who are you to say my life is not worth living?"

"I didn't ..." Jomon starts to say but then stops. He doesn't have to explain himself to these men.

"Plenty to live for," says another man. "Sure, this moment is rough. It's rough on all of us, but it won't last forever. Plenty of good things ahead."

"He doesn't see it that way," says Hi. "He thinks he's tossed his future in the garbage."

"Welcome to the club," says one of the other men.

Jomon squeezes himself up against the back wall, squishing his face into the cement blocks. He wishes he could just push himself right through them. He wishes they could swallow him up.

"You won't be in here forever," a man says. "You'll see the sun rise again. You'll be with your family again. Plenty to live for."

"Shut up," Jomon whispers. "Just shut up."

He hugs his knees to his chest and slumps against the wall. He stays that way until he gets a cramp in his back. He stretches out and turns himself around.

The boy from the other cell is sitting on the other end of Jomon's bed.

Jomon springs to his feet. "How did you get in here?"

"It's all right," says Hi. "Like I said, I'm your great-great-grandfather. I've got some things to tell you."

"I don't want to listen to anything you have to say," Jomon tells him. "Just leave me alone."

"All right," says Hi. He leans back against the wall and stares out the bars.

Slowly the evening darkens. The ceiling lights are bright in the hallway but Jomon, in the back of the cell, is in a shadow.

He is so tired. His eyelids droop, then close. Sleep finally begins to swirl around him.

Chatter monkeys in the trees
Swaying branches in the breeze
Sleep the hours of dark away
Wake up to a brighter day.

In an instant, Jomon is back on his feet and his hand is around the other boy's throat.

"Who taught you that?" Jomon spits in Hi's face. "That's the Soothing Song. That's my father's song. He wrote it. Who taught you that? Who are you?"

Hi breaks Jomon's clutch and sends him tumbling to the floor.

"I told you who I am," says Hi. "Do I really need to tell you again? I thought my great-great-grandson would be smarter than this. My father sang that song to me when I was small and I sang it to my boy. He sang it to his son. Your father sang it to you. And, if you don't kill yourself, you'll sing it to your child."

"You're my age," says Jomon.

"I know," replies Hi with a big grin. "It's great to be fifteen again, for however long it lasts. I'm here to tell you about my life."

"I told you, I don't want to listen."

"I'm here to tell you anyway." Hi's calmness is maddening.

"And then what?"

"I don't know."

Jomon tries to wriggle farther away from Hi but, of course, there is nowhere to go. His wriggling only makes him feel foolish, so he stops.

"I don't want to hear it," he says again. "I'm not listening."

"Listen or not, that's up to you," says Hi. "I'm going to tell you anyway. You should be thanking me. I would love to be able to talk to my great-great-grandfather. I'll bet he has all kinds of things to say."

"Then why didn't he come instead of you?"

"For a very good reason," says Hi. "I came because I'm the first suicide."

9

Great-Great-Grandfather's Contribution

I loved your great-great-grandmother the moment I saw her.

I was only ten years old at the time, but I knew it was love. I knew it deep in my soul, like I know my own name.

The first time I saw her, the sun was going down. I was in the cane field not far from Georgetown. I was there with my daddy and his friends, all sugar workers. I worked in sugar, too, alongside the men, although I was too small and scrawny to do the work of men. The workday was over. Our machetes were down and we were sitting around a fire, eating some fish I'd caught. I always kept a fishing line in my pocket. Made the hook myself.

Anyway, I was so proud that they were eating my food! They all had places to go, but they delayed their journeys to sit with Daddy and me and eat the fish I'd caught and cleaned and cooked.

The men were kidding me about my size, saying I couldn't be ten, I didn't look a day over six. I didn't mind them teasing. I knew they weren't being mean. Calling me six years old got them talking about when their fathers were six, back in 1834. That was the year of emancipation, when all the slaves were freed and there were big celebrations on all the plantations.

Except it was a lie. Anyone six years old and over was still a slave for four more years if they worked in the house, and six more years if they worked in the field.

Lies, lies, lies.

Of course, people were mad. They went on strike. Hundreds of people refused to go back to the fields and went into a church instead. They raised up their own flag, declared their own freedom. The government sent troops. A friend of my grandfather's, a man named Damon, was hanged for refusing to be a slave. If he were here today, he'd sure tell you to smarten up.

As the sun went down and we ate our fish, along the track by the sugar field walked a Chinese family, looking like they had just arrived in Guyana. We were used to seeing Chinese people because after the slaves became free they didn't want to work on the plantations any more for the men who enslaved them. Why would they? They left the sugar fields and started their own little farms and villages, sometimes on old plantations.

So the government imported people from India, Portugal, Ireland, Scotland and China to be indentured servants, which was a little better than slavery but not much. Those who came were desperate. Things were hard at home. They agreed to come to Guyana but then spent years working for next to nothing to pay off their passage and other debts to the landowners.

This family that I saw, there was a man and a woman and six children plus a baby. They looked like they were wearing most of the clothes they owned. Everyone had bundles. Overdressed, in the heat, looking tired beyond tired, they were moving so slowly I didn't think they would ever get to where they were going.

In the middle of this family, I saw my wife-to-be. The most beautiful girl. The rest of the family looked exhausted, bent under the weight of their journey and their belongings. But this girl was not bent. She looked at everything! She saw everything! The sky turning the color of cannonball flowers, the insects, the birds flying into the trees to shelter for the night. She saw all of it.

And she saw me. She looked at us around the cook fire and she did not look away.

Maybe you've never been looked at as if you were not there, but I have. You get so you expect it. So when someone actually sees you and does not scrunch up their nose or look away, oh, my great-great-grandson, that is like God himself is smiling down on you from heaven.

I stood up. I left my father and his friends to their memories and I carried my leaf full of cooked fish right over to her. I held it out to her.

Her father said some words I didn't understand. I learned later that he was telling her not to take food from a boy she didn't know.

She didn't listen to him. There was just enough light left in the sky for me to see the laughter in her eyes as she helped herself to a morsel of fish.

She chewed and smiled. Within moments my dinner was gone, spread among the little hands of many children.

I sensed movement around me. My father and his friends joined me on the path and were holding out their fish, too!

Finally, the mother and the father took bites of fish, nodded their thanks and then the family went on their way.

To this day I remember my father's arm around my shoulder and the pride in his voice when he said to his friends, "My son is a kind man."

Years went by. There was a growing Chinese community in Georgetown and I asked a rice grower to teach me some of his language. I kept my eye out for the girl. Her family opened an odd-goods shop. This shop happened — with a bit of detouring — to be on the same route I took to the field every day. My father walked the extra half-mile with me instead of going the shorter route, no matter how tired he was.

Every morning I would nod to the girl's father and say, "Good morning," in his language, and every night I would nod again and say, "Good night." My father did it with me.

At first we got no reaction. But who could resist my charms forever?

Sometimes I was rewarded with a glimpse of the girl. This wouldn't happen often. She was kept busy inside the shop and in the rooms they lived in behind it, but sometimes she would be outside with some of the younger children. I learned that her name was Lien. It means lotus. On mornings that I saw her, I just floated through my work. It was like my back didn't hurt and the cane juice didn't stick and attract flies to my skin.

In a world where she existed, nothing was ugly.

I started helping her father with odd jobs on my way back home from the cane fields at the end of the day. That shop sold everything — groceries, dry goods, tools, household things. There were always bundles to unpack, things to carry, shelves to stock. I made myself useful. I always worked hard, never asked for anything in return. I was just happy to be around her. My Chinese got pretty good. I taught English to them so they could serve their customers better. Lien picked up English very quickly. She was smart as well as beautiful.

Finally, her father and mother gave their consent and Lien and I got married. Such a beautiful little wedding! A bit of Buddha, a bit of Jesus, lots of love. I was so happy! Helped by my father and his friends, I built us a little house in Georgetown. I had just a little slip of land but I could work, there were fish in the river and we had everything we needed.

My wife and I had a son. Your great-grandfather. Of course he was perfect! Between Lien, her mother and my mother, I had to almost fight to get a chance to hold him. But I didn't mind. We were growing our family. We were building Guyana. There was nothing ahead of us but good times.

My Lien still helped her parents at their shop from time to time. She took the baby while he was still small. When he started walking and getting into things, my mother was only too happy to look after him when Lien and I were both working.

My son was barely two years old. Lien left him with my mother and went to the shop while I went to work in the field.

We heard a big explosion. It went on and on, bang after bang. We were out in the field. We heard the sounds but had no way of knowing what they meant. I did not know anything was wrong until I saw my mother, holding my son, standing next to a mound of chopped sugar cane.

My wife's parents stored fireworks in the back of their shop. Something went wrong. The whole shop blew up. My wife blew up with it. My beautiful Lien, my lotus flower, became a star. There was nothing left of her to bury.

I kept on living, one day after another, one breath after another, until my son was seventeen. Then I couldn't go on any longer. My son was raised. He was a man. I thought he didn't need me anymore. It was time for me to be with my wife.

So I killed myself.

The moment I did it, I wished I hadn't.

But by then I was dead.
It was too late to change my mind.

———

Hi stops talking, then adds one more thing.

"I thought my boy was grown up at seventeen. But you're fifteen. You're still a boy. Maybe my son was still a boy, too."

Hi shakes his head, sighs a long sigh and slides from the bed to the floor. He rests his arms on his knees and stares at the ground.

In the silence, Jomon takes a closer look at this strange boy.

He sees that Hi is wearing clothes that look like they came from a history book drawing of cane workers. Hi's trousers are made from some sort of coarse fabric. They stop mid-calf. His sandals are of crude leather with hemp-rope straps. His shirt is a wide-armed tunic also of coarse weave, long and loose.

Jomon notices other things, too, like the familiar shape of Hi's forehead and the shape of his chin.

Hi said his full name is Hiram Jomon Fowler.

Jomon's full name is Jomon Hiram Fowler.

10

Gather finally finds some green.

The world outside the museum is a strange one. The air still tastes of the sea and the jungle, like it did when Gather first walked this earth. The air also tastes of bitter smoke and the smells of human beings, the same breed of creature who hunted her down when she was first alive.

Her first day back to life has been difficult. At night, there were shadows she could slip into and walls she could hide behind. When the sun came up, the world filled with humans.

They make so much noise! They put the howler monkeys to shame. The humans also move fast in those hard shells they ride around in.

Gather needs to stay away from the humans. Most of the time, they pay no attention to her. She uses her sitting-still skills to hide in plain sight. Mostly the humans move past her, not seeing her, too busy hunting something else. Now and then a tiny human will point up at her and make some noise, but they get pulled away by a bigger human, too busy to stop and see.

It has been a long, hard day for Gather, trying to find a peaceful place to sit.

Finally, she finds the park.

There is a fence around the park, but that is no barrier for someone as big as Gather. She is over it in a jiffy. Then she is in the trees and the green. The grass is shorter than she remembers it, and the trees are sparser than they should be, but the place is earthy and soft and smells good. There are no cannonball trees in the park, but she finds bougainvillea flowers to eat and water in a pond to drink. She fills her belly, then shuffles into a lovely cool spot under a group of trees and settles in there to rest out of the heat.

Visitors come to the park and stand very close to Gather but they do not see her. They are there to get their picture taken next to the nearby statue of Gandhi, a Guyanese hero because he stood up to tyranny.

They see what they are prepared to see.

They are not ready to see anything else.

11

"Hurry up and wait."

Jomon hears the words from one of the adult prisoners from down the corridor.

"That's what court mornings are. Hurry up and then do nothing, for hours and hours and hours. Then hurry up again and come back here and do nothing again, for hours and hours and hours."

Jomon discovers that this is true. While the little window still shows darkness outside, the officers clang into the lockup, yelling orders to "Rise and shine" and "Get ready for court." Breakfast is shoved through the bars — one pine tart each. Hi and Jomon are handcuffed with their hands in front of them and then shackled together. They are the first ones loaded into the van. The adult prisoners who also have court dates are loaded in after them.

"Which one of you babies wanted to kill himself?" one of the adult prisoners asks.

Hi nods his head toward Jomon.

The adult prisoner extends a handcuffed hand, and with it, the hand of his neighbor, as close as he can get it to Jomon's face. He looks like a wild beast, able to chomp Jomon's head off with one bite.

"I'm glad to see you, son," he says. "I don't like anybody, and nobody likes me, but I am glad to see you here this morning. Got that?"

Jomon nods. "Yes," he says. Then he adds, because he means it, "Thank you."

Inside the courtroom, Jomon and Hi are put on a bench by themselves. The adult prisoners are made to crowd in together on a separate bench.

Jomon is scared. He has never been in trouble, never even been called down to the principal's office.

He wishes he'd managed to kill himself when he had the chance.

"No, you don't," says Hi, hearing his thoughts.

"Shut up," says Jomon.

Officer Grant comes over to him.

"Is there anything you want to say to me this morning, Jomon?" she asks.

Jomon finds himself wanting to ask her if she made her kids breakfast again, and what they had, but instead he just shakes his head.

Officer Grant looks at him for a long moment, then leaves him alone.

"All rise," the bailiff says. Shackles jangle as the prisoners stand. The judge enters and takes her place. Jomon keeps his eyes down, looking at her only when permission is given for everyone to sit.

The judge is old. Maybe she will be kind, like a grandmother. Maybe she'll let him offer to pay for the window, write an apology letter to the liquor-store owner, then walk out of the courtroom, back to ...

Back to what?

What is there now?

Jomon is so troubled by the question that he misses his name when it is called.

Hi elbows him in the ribs. "Answer her, man. How much trouble do you want?"

Jomon stands quickly, his chains rattling. "I'm sorry, your honor."

"Are we keeping you from something?" the judge asks.

"No, your honor. Nothing," he says, then adds a second, "I'm sorry."

The prosecutor reads out the charges. "This young man was arrested beside the liquor store on Waterloo Street on Friday night, late. He was next to a window that was broken, and evidence was recovered from inside the store that belongs to him. In addition, he resisted arrest and assaulted a police officer."

"A busy night, young man," says the judge. "How old are you?"

"Fifteen," mumbles Jomon.

"I can't hear you."

"Fifteen, your honor," Jomon repeats in a louder voice.

"Don't mumble in my courtroom, son," the judge says. "Mumbling wastes my time. If anyone's time is going to be wasted today, it's going to be yours, not mine. Understand? Who is responsible for you?"

Jomon has nothing to say to that.

"Are you thinking of mumbling again?" the judge asks.

"No, your honor."

"Are you planning on answering my question?"

Jomon remains silent. Officer Grant steps forward.

"May I address the court?" she asks the judge. The judge nods. "We have been unable to track down Jomon's father. His mother is deceased. He has refused to give us the names of any other family members."

"Jomon, where is your father?" the judge asks.

Jomon looks full at the judge. He can feel his muscles tense.

"Just put me back in jail," he says. "Just do it."

He doesn't know if he is daring her or begging. He doesn't care. What is the point of him hanging around this stupid courtroom in front of these strangers? No point. They should put him away and let him get on with it.

The judge, the lawyers and Officer Grant talk back and forth, but Jomon stops listening. He sits down, tired of the whole thing, not caring how much his shackles rattle.

In a second the bailiff is at his side and he stands up again.

"Good decision to get back on your feet, young man," the judge says. "Since you have no guardian here and are unable or unwilling to assist us in finding the person responsible for you, I am sending you to the youth detention center. You will be there until your next court date at least. I suggest you start cooperating before then if you want to be out of custody again before you are eighteen. That's all. Next case."

12

Mrs. Simson is sitting on the bench in Gather's room, looking up at the space where her friend should be standing, willing Gather to come back.

The museum officials must have put her in storage. But how would that explain the footprints?

Her cleaning shift over, Mrs. Simson has nothing to do but sit and wait.

Go home, she tells herself. *You're being foolish. Go home.*

But she can't bring herself to leave Gather's room.

Her friend is out there and none of the officials seems to know about it, even though they are paid to be responsible.

It is up to her to tell them.

She leaves Gather's room, locking the door behind her, and climbs the stairs to the chief executive's office.

Her heart is racing.

She knows the chief executive officer is not God or even the president, but he is the highest person in the museum, and she, the cleaner, is the lowest. Her religion teaches her that all people are equal under heaven. She believes this, but she doesn't know if the chief executive believes this. She has never talked to him.

Today, she has to. Her friend is missing and something must be done. Who better to know what to do than the top person in the whole museum?

She pulls together all her courage, raises her hand and knocks on his door.

There is no answer.

She waits and she waits.

He might be in a meeting, or sleeping late, or on holiday. He might be in his office and just not answering the door.

Mrs. Simson can't wait all day.

In her cleaning uniform pocket she always carries a small notebook and a pen. It helps her keep track of cleaning supplies she needs to order and tasks she has to do.

In the hall outside the chief executive's office, she tears an empty page from her notebook. It takes a moment for her to decide what to write.

Then she has it. Six words that will say it all. Six words that will spur the officials into heroic action to ensure the safety and well-being of her best friend.

Gather has gone for a walk.

She slips the note under the chief executive's door, feeling proud that she has done what she can.

Then she goes back to Gather's room. She wants to be there if her friend comes back.

13

Jomon is led away and put into the back of a police car. An officer leans his back against the car and folds his arms.

Foolishly, Jomon tries to open the car door from the inside. Of course it will not open. The officer half-turns around. Jomon sees the smirk on his face.

Nothing to do but sit. At least he is alone. He is disappointed in himself to realize that he is shaking, but he tells himself that this is normal. It's just nerves.

It's temporary. As soon as he can, he'll kill himself, and all of this will go away.

He sits back in the seat and tries to breathe deeply, a calming exercise his geography competition coach taught the team to do before matches. He closes his eyes.

"I thought I was done."

Jomon jumps in his seat and opens his eyes. That annoying Hi is sitting beside him in the back seat of the police car.

"Go away," says Jomon.

"You go away," says Hi.

"Leave me alone," says Jomon. "I don't want you anywhere near me."

"I don't like this any more than you do," Hi says. "I was fine to come back and tell you my story, but if I'm going to be fifteen again, I sure don't want to spend my time locked up in jail."

"That's not my problem," says Jomon.

"Wake up, little boy," says Hi. "Where you go, I go. Just because you don't care what happens to you, we all have to pay the price? I told you my story, so smarten up! I don't want to be going to jail!"

Jomon is about to elbow Hi hard in the ribs when the officers get into the front seat of the car. The officer in the passenger seat turns around and frowns at them.

"We've got a bit of a drive ahead of us," he says. "Not too long, but long enough. If either of you says one word it will seem like the longest ride of your young lives. Understand?"

Both boys are silent.

"Can I get a 'Yes, sir'?"

"Yes, sir," Jomon and Hi reply, glaring at each other.

The officer turns back to the front and looks at them in the rearview mirror. "You two keep glowering like that, your faces will stick that way. You look alike. Are you brothers?"

"No!" they both exclaim.

The officer just laughs and then leaves them alone.

Jomon tries to get his mind ready for what might be waiting for him at the detention center. Then he shrugs it off. Whatever detention is like, he won't be around for long. As soon as he gets there, he'll start looking for a way to end his life.

"I'm watching you," Hi reminds him.

"And I'm watching you!" says the officer in the passenger seat. "You open your mouth again, you'll really have something to watch."

Hi frowns at Jomon. Jomon frowns back, then spends the rest of the drive looking out the window.

They drive through Georgetown, and Jomon sees people going to the market, old people walking slowly with their toddler grandchildren, tourists looking at street maps. He sees a city full of people not going to prison that day, a city full of people who have no worries, no cares, no sorrows.

"You think you're the only one with pain?" Hi whispers. "All these people have pain. And they get up every day and do their best."

The officer in the passenger seat turns around and is about to give them the business but is stopped by the sudden honking of many car horns.

There is a traffic jam. Jomon hears angry shouting.

"We'd better deal with this," the driver says to the other officer. They pull over to the side of the road and get out of the car. Jomon and Hi watch them head up the road to see what the problem is. They are locked in.

Jomon keeps his head turned firmly away from Hi. He keeps his eyes focused out the window.

Just before the traffic starts flowing again, he catches a glimpse of something large — really large — lumbering away into the trees. It is just a glimpse.

As the officers return to the car and the car drives away, Jomon isn't totally sure if he really saw anything at all.

They drive out of Georgetown and into the countryside. The houses and shops give way to green fields, stands of coconut palms and mangrove thickets.

Jomon rarely gets to travel. The geography team had one away match, at Patentia Secondary School, but that was not far from Georgetown. Other than that, he is always in the city.

He stares out the window of the police car, wanting the trees and flowers and glimpses of the ocean to settle deep into his brain. It reminds him of Jomonland when Jomonland was alive.

Guyana's "Land of Many Waters" offers up to Jomon river after river, stream after stream, and ponds full of giant lily pads as big across as a man is tall. He sees flashes of black and gray as long-legged wood storks rise out of the marshes and take to the sky.

Jomon glances over at Hi. Hi is also staring at the sights out his window.

"It's all so different," Jomon hears Hi whisper. "And we're moving so fast!"

They are, in fact, driving slowly behind a truck full of melons.

Hi turns his head, catches Jomon watching him and grins. Jomon turns back to his own window.

After an hour of driving, the police car turns into a driveway facing a high chain-link fence with strands of barbed wire strung across the top. The gate in front swings open and the car drives into the yard.

"Out," the officers order, and the boys wriggle themselves around in the car seat until they can swing their shackled legs through the door and push themselves off the seat back with their elbows. Everything is harder in chains and cuffs.

Jomon and Hi are marched toward the office. At the building's threshold is a large red mat with the word "Welcome" on it in big white letters.

"Two for you today," says their driver. The cuffs and the shackles are taken off.

"Trouble?" the warden asks. She comes out from behind her desk to greet them.

"Nothing you can't handle."

Jomon looks around the small office. Dark green walls, beige filing cabinets, a sofa they are not invited to sit on, and several guards doing paperwork and filling out a duty roster on a chalkboard nailed to the wall. Also on the walls is a photograph of Guyana's president and a tourism poster of Kaieteur Falls with the words "Largest Single Drop Waterfall in the World" printed across the top.

Jomon has never been to the famous waterfall, but he wishes he could be there right now, standing on a rock, feeling the spray and breathing the fresh air.

When all this is over, I'll go, Jomon thinks.

Then he remembers that he's planning on killing himself at his first opportunity. He has a flash of regret that he'll never see the falls.

"See? You haven't even died yet and already you're regretting it," says Hi.

Jomon is more than a little tired of Hi hearing his thoughts and is glad when a guard comes right over to Hi, stands three inches from him and says, "Did someone invite this boy to talk? I don't remember that."

The warden finishes with the paperwork. "Any health issues?" she asks.

"This one's got some cuts on his feet," an officer says. "They got freshly bandaged this morning. He'll live."

That's what you think, thinks Jomon.

Hi lands a quick, small kick to Jomon's shin, a kick that is not noticed by the guards.

"Time to explain the rules," the warden says, "and you'd better listen. No fighting. You fight, you go to solitary. We don't care who starts it. No fighting, no cursing, no talking back. Do as you're told and don't argue. Stay out of the girls' dormitory. Keep your hands off the other detainees, and I mean it. No slugs, no hugs. Got it?"

"Yes, ma'am."

The warden points toward a big cardboard box on the floor in the corner.

"Get yourself a new shirt and some shoes," she says.

Jomon easily finds some sandals that fit him, but most of the shirts are smaller sizes.

"We don't mind waiting for you," says the warden.

Jomon grabs the first T-shirt that looks big enough. He takes off his bloody, soiled school uniform shirt and puts on the T-shirt. The warden points to a garbage bin for his old shirt.

"What do you say when you are given something?" she asks.

"Thank you," Jomon says, and he truly is grateful.

"Take them in," the warden instructs one of the guards.

A guard nods his head toward a stack of bed sheets. Jomon and Hi pick up their allotment and follow the guard out of the office and across the yard to another building.

"This is the boys' dormitory," the guard says. "Pick a cot. Make up your bed. Be quick."

The narrow cots are crowded in. There are two cots in the room that don't already have sheets on them. They are next to each other. Jomon is annoyed that there won't be more distance between him and Hi. He is also surprised to find he's relieved. At least he'll be sleeping next to someone who won't hurt him. Hi does not make Jomon feel afraid.

Jomon gets to work making up his own bed. He's done this ever since he was small. His mother insisted that he know how to do all the things that needed doing around the house, from cooking to cleaning to fixing things that break.

He gets the bed made in no time.

"I gave you an order," Jomon hears.

He looks up to see the guard standing over Hi. Hi is not making his bed. He's holding the sheets, looking confused.

"Are you refusing to do what you're told?"

"He isn't," Jomon says. He takes a sheet from Hi. "I'll help him."

He unfolds a sheet and nods to Hi to do the same.

"We each get our own bed?" Hi asks in a whisper.
Jomon nods as he stuffs the pillow in a case.
"This is a really nice place, isn't it?"
Jomon doesn't know what to say.
"You're done?" the guard asks. "Good. Move."
He shepherds them out of the dorm, down the stairs
and out to the yard.

14

The yard is a small, barren space between the buildings, in full view of the large office window and the awning that covers the area where the guards sit. The ground is dirt and gravel.

Jomon hears the muffled sounds of a classroom coming from a room above them. When he closes his eyes, he can almost imagine he is back in his own school.

There would have been an announcement that morning, congratulating the geography team on their win. Maybe there was even a special assembly. His school has never won before. The whole school would have clapped for his teammates, and everyone would probably know what Jomon had done and why he wasn't there.

Jomon sits in the dirt with his back against a wall. Someone has drawn little circles in the dirt. Jomon pitches pebbles into the circles, trying to make bullseye.

Crash!

Jomon jumps to his feet, looking for the source of the noise. The guards haven't moved. No one else seems bothered by the sound. Jomon wonders if he's losing his mind.

"Relax. It's just a cannonball tree," says Hi. "Haven't you heard that before?"

"I'm from the city."

"Well, you'll hear a lot of them out here," Hi says. "Look." He points to a large stand of tall, pink-flowered trees across the road from the detention center.

As Jomon watches, a large, round seed pod breaks free and crashes to the ground.

"Smell that?" Hi asks. "Perfume from the flowers and rot from the seeds. You can't mistake that smell for any other."

Jomon sits back in his spot and returns to his pebble pitching. Hi sits beside him. Jomon doesn't have the energy to move or tell Hi to get lost.

"This would be a good day for fishing," Hi says. "Do you do much fishing?"

"No," says Jomon. "Never."

"Never been fishing? What do you eat?"

Jomon doesn't answer. He feels like all the fight has drained out of him. He doesn't even have the energy to look around for ways to kill himself. At this moment, even suicide seems too hard. He wishes he could just fade away.

"Maybe that's why I'm still here," says Hi. "To take you fishing. I thought it was to tell you my story, but maybe I'm supposed to take you fishing. Then whenever you feel like dying, you'll tie a line to a stick and go sit by the water and you'll feel better."

"Really?" asks Jomon. "Fishing? That's your answer?"

Hi shrugs. "Why not?"

"Didn't help you, did it," Jomon says nastily. He gets up and walks away.

Hi doesn't follow him. Jomon goes to the other end of the yard and looks back. Hi is still on the ground, staring at the dirt, and for a brief moment, Jomon wants to do something to make him feel better.

Just then, he hears music coming from the classroom. The young inmates are singing.

> *This little light of mine,*
> *I'm gonna let it shine.*

They sing through a few verses, including some Jomon's never heard before.

This good brain of mine,
I'm gonna let it shine.

Jomon's mum used to sing that song with him. It was one of her favorites. She'd add her own lyrics, too: "This fine boy of mine, he's gonna really shine." And, "These dirty dishes of mine, Jomon's gonna make them shine."

Moments after the song ends, the classroom door opens. The rest of the prisoners flow down the stairs and into the yard. They look at Jomon and Hi with mild curiosity.

Jomon is surprised at how young many of them are. A few of them don't look any older than ten. They all look ordinary. Put school uniforms on them and they could be his classmates.

It's not what he is expecting. He thought they'd look tough and mean, but they just look like kids.

"It's you," Hi says, almost like a breath. "It's you! It's really you!"

Jomon looks at Hi and then at the boy Hi is talking to. The boy is his age, with a face messed with confusion and sadness and Jomon can't tell what else.

Hi takes a step toward the boy and then another step.

"Don't," Jomon warns. He's seen enough prison movies and schoolyard fights to know that you don't walk up to someone when you're talking nonsense. "Don't."

Hi ignores him.

"Dev," says Hi, getting closer and closer to the boy who is now starting to back away. Jomon can almost see horror in the boy's face. "Dev, it's so good to see you! Don't you recognize me? It's me!"

Dev's face now shows recognition and pure rage.

"You!" growls Dev, first low in his chest, then louder, a scream from his heart. "You!"

"Yes!" exclaims Hi. "It's me! We're together again!"

Dev plows himself headfirst into Hi's stomach. Hi hits the ground and Dev rolls on top of him, crying and pounding him with both fists.

Jomon tries to pull the boys apart, but Dev's anger is making him strong and fearless. Jomon quickly gets lost in a tangle of swinging arms and flying fists.

The fight doesn't last long. Guards pull them apart.

"No fighting!" a guard yells. "Solitary!"

"I was trying to stop them!" Jomon protests.

The guards don't care. Jomon is force-marched with Hi and Dev through the yard and around the corner. They end up in front of a small brick shed with a series of narrow doors across the front. Three of the doors are open. The three boys are tossed inside, with Jomon in the middle.

The doors are slammed shut and then bolted.

Jomon is in a space not much bigger than an outhouse. The only light comes from the grill in the door.

There is a tattered straw mat on the cement floor. Jomon sits on it and hugs his knees to his chest.

"What just happened?" he cries.

"Jomon," says Hi, from the cell to his right. "Let me introduce you to Angel Liang Fowler. Your great-grand-father."

"I hate you!" shouts the boy in the cell on Jomon's left. "I could kill you!"

"You're too late for that," Hi shouts back. "I'm already dead. And so are you."

"What just happened?" Jomon hollers again.

One moment, he was sleeping on his bed, exhausted from an evening of competition and forced celebration. He was feeling empty, but that wasn't unusual. He was already making plans to fill the emptiness with exams and jobs. They weren't great plans, but his expectations weren't very high. He would have made them work.

The next moment, he was running down the street without shoes, breaking windows and being slammed against a police car. Now he is stuck in a cell between a kid who calls himself Jomon's great-great-grandfather and another boy who the first kid says is Jomon's great-grandfather.

Jomon wants none of it. He wants out.

He bangs on the door, rattles the bars on the tiny window and calls out, "Open this damn door!"

"I'll pay for the window," he shouts. He has no

money, but he'll figure out a way. "I'm sorry I broke it.
Now, LET ME OUT OF HERE!"

Part of a face suddenly appears at the small window.

"Stop that," the part-face says. "You shout again, I'll
keep you in longer."

Jomon bends over and pounds his thighs with his
fists. All he accomplishes is to bruise his legs and his
hands and to wear himself out.

The unfairness, the rottenness of it all!

He stretches out on his back on the straw mat and
watches the sliver of sky through the little window.
Sometimes a cloud passes by. Sometimes an egret trail-
ing its long legs.

Every few minutes, the part-face of a guard blocks
out the sky as he peers into Jomon's cell. Bread and
water are delivered. The sky changes from bright blue
to gray to black. Jomon slaps at mosquitoes. He keeps
breathing in and out. He has no other choice.

The sounds of the detention center go quiet. There is
silence except for the cries of owls and the buzz of cicadas.

Jomon doesn't even try to sleep.

Deep into the night, another sound reaches his ears.

It comes from the cell belonging to Dev, the boy Hi
called Jomon's great-grandfather.

It is a soft sound, muted by the thick brick walls of
the solitary compound. But the night is quiet and even
a soft sound can be heard.

The boy in the cell next to Jomon is crying.

Jomon puts his hand on the cell wall, as if that can comfort the boy who is feeling as sad and alone as Jomon. The boy's tears are contagious. Jomon feels like crying now, too.

"Sing the Soothing Song," he hears the boy say. "Sing the Soothing Song."

Jomon wonders if the boy is talking to him, but then the boy himself starts to sing.

> *Chatter monkeys in the trees*
> *Swaying branches in the breeze*
> *Sleep the hours of dark away*
> *Wake up to a brighter day.*

Singing it once isn't enough. The boy starts to sing it a second time. Jomon joins in, and, from the other side of his cell, he hears Hi join in, too.

They sing the song five times before they are soothed enough to slip into sleep.

15

"How long are we going to be locked up in here?" Jomon asks the guard who delivers their breakfast.

"Do you have someplace else to be?" the guard asks before she closes the door on him.

Jomon thinks that is kind of a mean answer, but he doesn't say so. What would be the point?

They are allowed to empty out their slop buckets and to mop out their cells. The few minutes of sun feels good.

When Jomon goes back in his cell, it smells of Dettol. The dampness makes the air inside feel heavy. He goes back to sitting. There is nothing else to do.

Jomon falls asleep after lunch. He is woken up by a voice outside.

"Solitary means alone."

"I am well aware of the definition. You tell me every time I bring my students down here for a class."

Jomon gets up from the floor and goes to his small window.

A tall, older man in a crisp white shirt is directing the young prisoners to place chairs in a semicircle in the yard, facing the cell doors. A guard is there, too, watching them and frowning.

"Take those chairs back up to the schoolroom," she orders.

"Guard Boyton, I assure you, all the chairs will go back to their proper places at the end of the lesson time."

"The chairs are supposed to stay in that room."

"Show me the regulation," the tall man sighs, as though he has been through this before. "I am happy to show you the regulation that says all children are entitled to an education. All children means all. Even those in solitary. All we are doing is moving the classroom down here so that the boys in solitary can be educated."

"They are being punished," says the guard.

"Yes, they are," agrees the teacher.

Jomon watches the guard frown again and she warns the children, "Any of you cause trouble down here, you'll have to deal with me."

She turns and walks away.

"Students," says the teacher, "Guard Boyton and

I just had a disagreement. Did we say mean things to each other?"

"No," say the inmates.

"Did we use curse words?"

"No."

"Did anybody hit anybody?"

"No."

"Very good," says the tall man. "We are learning great things today. When you speak with Guard Boyton, I want you all to use your good manners. Good manners keep us calm, and they teach others how we want to be treated. Do I have your promise on that?"

"Yes," they all promise.

"Now, let's take our seats and get on with our lesson."

The teacher turns to the cell doors holding back Jomon, Hi and Dev. "I know one of you gentlemen already. I look forward to meeting you two new boys when your time in solitary is done. For today's lesson, we are going to work on our skills at reading out loud. I will begin."

He asks if everyone is comfortable. Everyone is. He settles into a chair, opens a book and begins to read.

"Marley was dead, to begin with. There is no doubt whatever about that."

Jomon almost laughs.

He knows this book.

It's *A Christmas Carol* by Charles Dickens. It's the story of a man who is taught important lessons by ghosts who come to visit him.

Of course that would be the book!

Jomon marvels at the weirdness of it all, then forgets about it as he gets caught up in the story. The teacher reads the first few pages, then passes the book to a small girl. The girl falters as she reads, but no one seems to mind.

Jomon sure doesn't.

It is just really, really nice being read to.

Later that night, after everyone is in bed and the night guards are quiet in their office, Jomon hears his name.

"Jomon? You still there?"

It's Dev.

"I'm here," Jomon replies.

"I have to talk to you," Dev says.

"Okay."

"I'm so mad at my father. I don't want to talk to him. But I do want to talk to you. I need to talk to you."

"I'm listening," Jomon says.

"I've been waiting for you," Dev says. "I don't like being here. I need to tell you my story, then maybe I can move on."

"Move on where?"

"I don't know. Out of here, at least. Can I tell you my story? Do you have time now?"

Jomon thinks that is a ridiculous question, but he answers anyway.

"Now is perfect," he says.

The boy in the cell next to him takes a deep breath and begins.

16

Great-Grandfather's Contribution

My name is Angel Liang Fowler. People call me Dev. Short for Devil. My relatives all said, "That's no angel, that's a devil." So they called me Dev. You can call me Dev, too. I don't like it but I'm used to it.

I was just a baby when my mother died in the fireworks explosion.

I don't like fireworks, or any loud sounds. I can handle the cannonball fruit exploding because it's nature and I grew up with it. But any loud human sounds? I don't like them.

My mother died and there I was — squawking, colicky, not a good baby. A good baby is one who is quiet and sleeps all the time. A good child is one that no one ever hears from. Who decided that? If I could go back, I'd make more noise, not less. What did being quiet ever get me? And the truth is, even if I had been a better baby, they still wouldn't have wanted me.

My mother's parents didn't want me because I didn't look enough like my mother. My father's family didn't want me because I looked too much like my mother. And my father didn't want me because he wanted to feel sorry for himself more than he wanted to take care of me.

I know this is true because they all told me to my face. To others, they'd say I was too much trouble, or I'd be better off in town instead of in the village. But to me, they'd say, "You have too much Chinese in your face." Or, "Your skin is so dark. Your mother's skin was beautiful and yours is so ugly." My father would just look at me and say, "Take him away." And he'd open a bottle of rum and take a long drink.

Back and forth I went, between my mother's family and my father's family. I picked up some schooling. Taught myself, mostly. One of the old men in the neighborhood took me under his wing, coached me in arithmetic and grammar, got me ready for high school. He said we owed it to our slave ancestors to become educated because they couldn't be.

I think maybe his eyesight wasn't so good and he couldn't see how worthless I was. That's why he was so kind to me. Or maybe he was just a kind man. I'm hoping to get the chance to ask him when all of this is over.

I spent most of my childhood away from my father. He would pop around every now and then, and I'm pretty sure he gave my relatives money to help feed me and all that, but he never spent any time with me.

Then, when I was ten or so, Dad got religion.

He'd had a bad bout of drinking. He was lying in some street, swimming in vomit and his own pee. As he told it later to anyone who would listen, he looked up and saw an angel from God. She was dressed all in white. She told him, "Jesus loves you," and he was all healed.

He wasn't, but you've figured that out already.

This angel was really a human woman. She was with the Jordanites. Are they still around? They dressed all in white and held services out in the open, like on Bourda Green or Stabroek Market square. They preached on street corners, too. That's how my father got involved. He was passed out drunk on the corner where they wanted to hold a service.

They treated Dad really well, those Jordanites. They helped him get sober. They cleaned him up and fed him and found him a decent room to live in. He got saved and then he came and got me from my relatives' house.

THE GREATS

There were no books in my father's relatives' house except for the Bible. To get me out of their way, Dad's relatives would say, "Go sit in the corner and learn a Bible verse." I learned a lot of Bible verses!

When my father saw how many verses I knew, and how easy it was for me to learn them, he bought me a white suit and paraded me out at services. And I liked it! People didn't care that I was ugly. They cheered when I quoted Colossians 3:2 or Luke 10:19, or whatever they wanted to hear.

But Dad got thirsty again. He needed money for drink so he got the brilliant idea of using me to get it. Away from the Jordanites who had saved his sorry life, he put me out on the street in my white suit to quote Bible verses and collect money like a trained parrot. He'd tell people the money was for the Lord, but he spent it on bottles.

I knew it was wrong. I was happy to be with my father when it looked like he really wanted to be with me, but as soon as I figured out that he was just using me, I was done. But I was a kid. What could I do? I started mumbling my Bible verses so people wouldn't pay much. That just got him mad.

In the end, Dad was his own undoing. He got thirstier and thirstier and needed more money than I could bring in.

One day I woke up to find that he'd sold my white suit and everything else I had, except for the skivvies that I wore to bed. He laid in a stock of hooch and yelled at me to get out.

So I left, in nothing but my underwear.

I slept in the tool shed at the school. The caretaker gave me a pair of trousers and a shirt. I exchanged work for food. I managed to get my diploma. No one came to watch me graduate. I took my diploma home to show my father. He was dead. Killed himself. He'd been dead for some time. The flies were terrible.

I was seventeen.

Flies and fireworks. I hate them both.

The next years blurred by. I worked. I did every job I could find. Moved cargo on the docks, cut sugar cane, cleaned out ditches that were clogged with mud and sewage. Hot, nasty work! It was the Depression, which hit Guyana like it hit every place, but there was work for those willing to sweat and suffer. And then the war started. More work for more people. Easier work. Better paying. For a time, I guarded boats loaded with bauxite before they were shipped out to the United States. Bauxite was used in making fighter planes. All kinds of work. I saved my money.

I married your great-grandmother in 1942. Her name was Indra, and I knew her from school. She was very smart. Could have run the country. Should have run the country. She proposed to me! I was astonished that she asked, and because of that, I said yes, even though I probably shouldn't have. I wanted to love her, and I acted like I did. Maybe I did love her. I was always kind to her. I never drank. I knew how to behave. But deep down in me there was a pit of loneliness, and I didn't know how to get out of it.

A year after we were married, we had a son, Barnabas. He was your grandfather.

Indra's family was from India. They came to Guyana several generations before, as indentured servants. When Barnabas was a baby, there was famine in Bengal. Indra and I joined a committee to bring people from the famine zone to Guyana. It was a lot to take on, but we knew how to work, and to work for something good. Well, we were young. It made us happy. It was good.

The newcomers from Bengal brought with them terrible stories of starvation, of animals and people dying in the streets. Some also brought leprosy.

Leprosy was already in Guyana. It was everywhere. But we think my wife caught it from the people she was helping. It wasn't their fault. They didn't know they had it.

First she got white patches on her skin. She ignored them. She was busy. She cared for our son and so many people, and leprosy never crossed her mind.

Eventually, she couldn't ignore it any longer. She went to the doctor. He sent her to live in the leprosy hospital in Mahaica. Our son was raised by the nuns in the Lady Denham home just outside the gates of the hospital. It was a home for the healthy children of leprosy patients. The children who had leprosy lived in other homes, inside the fence.

I stayed behind in Georgetown. I had just gotten a good job, assisting a shipping supervisor at the dockyards, and we thought Indra would get better and come home. I worked hard and spent very little money on myself. I visited almost every month. Each time I did, I took presents. Indra liked those little tins of peppermints, and white nightgowns with yellow ribbons. Barnabas got toys and new clothes, although I don't think he liked them. I often saw other children wearing the clothes and playing with the toys.

Sometimes I helped out the nuns by doing small repairs around the grounds, painting sheds, installing new window screens. Barnabas followed me around, helping when he could, talking, talking, talking. He didn't notice that I never knew what to say to him. How does a father talk to his child? Mine almost never talked to me.

Barnabas didn't notice. He was happy doing all the talking and telling joke after joke. The jokes weren't always funny, but I always laughed. It was something I could do for him.

Later, when his mother passed away, he came back to Georgetown to live with me. He had no jokes left. I didn't know how to help him find new ones. I didn't know how to help him do anything.

I tried to be a better father to my son than my father was to me. I tried to let him know he was important. I tried to keep him safe. But I wasn't there for large parts of his life, and I don't think he ever forgave me. I should have taken a lesser-paying job closer to the leprosy hospital, so that I could see him every day.

My father failed me, and I failed my son.

The pressure of that failure pushed me down.

I waited until my son was far, far away.

Then I killed myself.

As soon as I did it, I wished I hadn't.

But by then I was dead.

It was too late to change my mind.

17

Jomon stays quiet for a long time after Dev finishes talking.

The only thing he says is, "I'm going to call you Angel."

He needs to think.

It's all so strange.

There is Hi's name, Hiram Jomon Fowler, so close to his own, Jomon Hiram Fowler. There is the way both Hi and Angel know the Soothing Song. They both look like him — the position of their ears, the shape of their foreheads and chins — and they seem to be able to read his thoughts.

Most strange of all is Angel's story. It is familiar to Jomon. Parts of it, anyway. He can't remember where he heard it, but he knows he's been told bits of this family story before.

Maybe they are just like Scrooge's *fragments of underdone potato*, when he first sees the ghost of Jacob Marley.

Or maybe they are real.

Jomon winds his fingers through the bars in the window and leans his head on the door.

They don't know me. If they knew me, they would know I'm not worth bothering about.

"Why aren't you?" asks Angel.

Jomon hears the voice right behind him. He turns to see Angel and Hi inside the cell with him. Angel is sitting as far away from Hi as possible, which isn't far in that small space.

"Why aren't you worth bothering about?" Angel asks again.

Jomon shakes his head.

"Just tell us," says Hi. "What makes you so unworthy? What horrible thing did you do?"

"It's what I didn't do!" Jomon spits out. He slumps to the floor with his back against the cell door.

"Tell us," says Hi.

Jomon can't get the words out.

"If you could do one thing better," Angel says. "What would it be?"

Jomon answers without hesitation. "I would say goodbye to my mother."

He starts to cry. He lowers his head, ashamed to be crying in front of the other two boys.

When he finally looks up again, he is all alone in the cell.

The sounds of the night take over, and Jomon sleeps.

18

"I think we can all agree we have a crisis on our hands."

The chief executive officer of the national museum looks from one official to the other.

They are all together in his office. He looks down at the note in his hand and reads it out loud.

"Gather has gone for a walk."

"I would rather call it an opportunity," says the marketing manager. She's the one who came up with the Name the Sloth contest.

"An opportunity to lose our jobs," says the head of security. He always wears dark glasses, even indoors. People assume he has a problem with his eyes, but he really wears them because he thinks they make him look like a TV detective. "If it gets out that we let an expensive exhibit be stolen right out from under our noses, we'll be in trouble."

"*You* will be in trouble," says the financial officer. "Why did you let the workers just cover that wall with plastic? Anyone could get in!"

"If you had released more money," says the security head, "we could have hired twice the workers and gotten the whole thing done in a day."

"I only release what I am authorized to release." She looks at the chief executive. "You're the one with the authority. It's your responsibility."

"That's right," says the security head. "And if you had approved my requests for armed guards and cameras and a pack of vicious dogs, we could have avoided this whole mess."

The marketing manager is enjoying herself. The lost sloth cannot in any way be blamed on her. Maybe her colleagues will all be fired and she could be the boss!

"*My* idea," she says, "is to have a Find the Sloth competition. This way, Gather's disappearance will look like a plan instead of carelessness. I'll have a press conference to announce it." She might have to go shopping for something special to wear on television.

"Impossible!" says the security head. "We must be sworn to secrecy. No one is to leave this room until …"

His sentence trails off. He remembers he has an appointment with his barber that afternoon.

"We have to do something," says the chief executive. "Gather is our most valuable exhibit. What are we going to do if our funders find out?"

"Maybe she wasn't stolen," says the financial officer. "What does that note say again? *Gather has gone for a walk?* Why not just say, *Gather is missing?* Maybe Gather really has gone for a walk."

"If that is even a remote possibility," the security head says, "then we had better be absolutely certain to keep it a secret. If we tell people there's a giant prehistoric sloth roaming around Guyana, there will be panic in the streets."

His voice is firm, but he is a little bit excited at the possibility of a nation-wide panic. He has a mental picture of himself standing on top of a tank, urging calm. He is not sure where he'll get an army tank, or what purpose it would serve in calming people down, but he likes the picture.

"I agree," says the chief executive. "No one else can know. We'll get the sloth back in the hall, repair the wall, and no one will be the wiser."

"The only people who know are the four of us," says the security head. "Plus the person who wrote the note. Who is she?"

"Calls herself Mrs. Simson," says the chief executive. "The cleaner."

"Fire her," says the security head.

"No, sell her on the secrecy, then give her a raise," says the marketing manager.

"Not too big a raise," says the financial officer.

"We'd better go talk to her," says the chief executive.

They all leave the office. There is some confusion at the door because the chief executive isn't sure whether it looks more powerful for him to go first or to make others go first, but they sort it out and tour the museum at a walk-run, looking for the cleaner.

"Why is the Gather exhibit closed?" asks a teacher with her first-grade students gathered around her like baby ducks.

The officials rush by without answering and are serenaded by six-year-olds chanting, "We want Gather! We want Gather!"

They go through the whole museum without finding Mrs. Simson. The only space left to check is Gather's room.

They head quickly to the door of the exhibit hall and pull it open.

Mrs. Simson is on the bench. She rises to her feet and looks squarely at the chief executive.

"Six words," she said. "It took you this long to read six words. Now what are you going to do to fix this?"

19

It's chore time at the detention center.

Young prisoners are bent over their brooms, sweeping the yard of leaves and debris so that snakes and scorpions have nowhere to hide. Other prisoners are wiping down railings, mopping floors and emptying trash cans.

Jomon, Hi and Angel were released from solitary earlier that morning. Jomon and a small girl named Cora are assigned to the Welcome mat.

"Clean off all that dust and dirt," says Guard Boyton. "I want it looking like new." She leaves them to it.

"I'd rather sweep," says Cora. "Sometimes the guards drop stuff. I found a pen once. All we get from this job is dust up our nose. What are you here for?"

Jomon doesn't see any reason not to tell her. "I broke a window."

"We have another window breaker here," she says. She looks around the yard and points to a boy in a white shirt. "That's Keith. He broke a school window."

"What did *you* do?" Jomon asks her. "You're what — eight?"

"Ten," says Cora. "I won't stay where I'm supposed to."

"Why not?"

"I like to move around. The mat goes here," she says, pointing to a railing.

Jomon hangs the mat where he's told. Cora hits it with the flat of her hand. Dirt flies out.

Jomon hits the mat like Cora does. They get a rhythm going. Slowly, the bright red and white letters emerge from the dirt. The mat is made of thick, coarse stuff. It stamps an imprint of tiny pinpricks on their palms.

They take a break to rub their hands. Jomon looks around for Angel and Hi. Cora wipes off the dirt that's landed on her T-shirt.

"One of your friends is with the sweepers," she says. "The other is cleaning the guards' toilet."

"You pay attention," Jomon says.

"I have to," says Cora. "I'm one of the smallest. Knowing things is important. Everyone has something they want to hide from the guards. I find out what that is, let the person know that I know, and then I keep my mouth shut. Unless."

"Unless someone bothers you," Jomon guesses.

"You catch on quick."

"I'm not going to bother you."

"Good."

They get back to work. Cora fills him in on the other kids.

"Zara, Gloria, Josephine and Esme are all runaways, like me. Most of the girls who come through here are runaways. Sometimes we get a girl thief, but not usually. You see that small boy sweeping by the fence? That's Angus. He helped his uncle break into houses. Uncle got away. Angus is here. Lucky, the long, skinny one? He beat his father with a fence post. Came in here with his face all punched-up so I'm guessing his father deserved it."

She keeps up the chatter while they finish. Their work passes inspection. They are allowed to put the mat back down in front of the office door.

They join the line of kids at the bottom of the staircase that leads to the schoolroom. Angel and Hi fall in behind them.

"Jomon, I cleaned the outhouse," says Hi. "But it was *inside* the house. If you press a handle, water rushes. Every time!"

"*He's* found an angle," says Cora. "He's acting weird, but funny weird, not scary weird. Kids will leave him alone because they're not sure what he'll do. He'll have to keep up the act, though."

Jomon doesn't think that will be a problem.

"What are we doing now?" Hi asks.

"School," says the boy called Lucky, who still has a scar under his left eye. "And shut up. The guards keep us standing here until we're all quiet."

"What do I do in there?" Jomon hears Hi whisper to Angel.

"Do what I do," Angel whispers back.

It hits Jomon that Hi has never been to school.

He files up the steps and into the classroom with the other young prisoners.

It is the strangest classroom he has ever seen. Two long tables, end to end, take up most of the space, with only a few feet on each side to give the kids room to move. At one end of the room there is a small desk for the teacher and a few shelves, mostly empty. Jomon sees the copy of *A Christmas Carol*, a few old math books, *A History of England*, with the cover half-torn, a box of mixed pens and pencil stubs, another of crayon bits and some stacks of paper.

The walls make up for the bare shelves. The yellow paint is almost completely covered with posters. Some are pictures cut out of magazines — dinosaurs, flowers, polar bears and the Taj Mahal.

Some of the posters are the ones the government sends round to all schools, about healthy nutrition, avoiding malaria, and being safe on the streets.

Most are hand-lettered signs with sayings like *You Can Do It!* and *The president of Guyana was once a child like you.* There are quotes by Nelson Mandela, Oprah Winfrey, Gandhi and Malala Yousafzai.

Everywhere Jomon looks, there is something interesting to see.

"Sit with me," Cora says.

He follows her around the table. He sits carefully. The seat is broken and he has to wriggle to keep from getting pinched. Sawdust spills out of the warped table onto his trousers.

The chairs fill up. Jomon counts twenty-four other kids. Angel is at the far end of the room. Hi, across from Jomon, is looking all around, his eyes wide.

"What does that say?" he asks, pointing at a sign behind Jomon.

Jomon twists around. *"You must do the thing you think you cannot do.* Eleanor Roosevelt."

Hi is already pointing at another sign.

"What about that one?"

"Women hold up half the sky."

"And that one, beside it?"

Jomon is about to read a quote from Helen Keller when the teacher walks into the classroom. Officer Grant is with him.

"Good morning, young scholars," he says. "We have a guest this morning."

Officer Grant waves hello. "Are you ready to do some learning today, young people? Your teacher tells me this is his smartest group ever."

The teacher probably says that about every group, Jomon thinks, but still, it's a nice thing to say.

"I'm here on a special delivery mission." Officer Grant takes an envelope out of her uniform pocket. "Jomon, you've got a letter."

The room is silent as she hands Jomon the envelope.

"I've never gotten a letter," says Cora. Heads shake all around the table. No one has ever gotten a letter. "What does it say?"

"It's Jomon's letter to share or not," says Officer Grant. To Jomon she says, "I've got fifteen minutes before I leave. I can take your reply with me, so you'd better read your letter now and get busy writing back."

All eyes on him, Jomon opens the envelope with his name on it and takes out a handmade card. He reads the front silently to himself.

For one thousand points, name three people who are wishing you well.

He opens the card. He reads the inside:

Brandon, Chandra and Reshma — teammates now and always.

P.S. We'll win again next year!

"I guess you're wrong about them not caring about you," says Angel.

"Yeah," says Hi. "Maybe you're wrong about other things, too."

The teacher passes a pen and a blank sheet of paper down to Jomon. Jomon picks up the pen but can't begin to form any words. He doesn't know how to respond to a message from his former life, a life that no longer belongs to him.

Officer Grant goes around the room, talking with the students. She asks about their schoolwork. She plays a hand of cards. She has personal messages for many of them.

"Your mother says to tell you she is feeling better," she says to one of the girls Cora told Jomon is a runaway. To a boy, she says, "I'm sorry, but your court date has been postponed again. They're looking at next week. I'll let you know as soon as they decide." To Angus, the small boy who helped his uncle break into houses, she says, "Your teacher tells me you memorized the names of all of Guyana's administrative regions in just one hour. And you told me you can't learn anything! You were fooling with me, weren't you?"

She kneels down beside Cora and says quietly, "It's not going to work out with your aunt in Hopetown. We'll have to think of something else."

"I told you they don't want me," says Cora. "I don't want them, either."

Officer Grant wipes a tear off Cora's cheek.

"You leave this with me," she says. "Your job is to do your schoolwork. Get Jomon to help you. He's good at answering questions."

At the end of fifteen minutes, she says to Jomon, "Time's up. I have to get back to work. Is your letter done?"

He looks from the police officer to the blank piece of paper and back to the officer again.

"Words get stuck in the pen sometimes," she says gently. "Is there anything you would like me to say to them?"

Jomon's first instinct is to shake his head, but he doesn't. Instead, he says, "Please tell them thank you."

Officer Grant smiles at him and nods. "I'll do that."

Jomon's eyes flicker at the nearly empty bookshelves.

"Something else?" Officer Grant asks him.

"He wants you to ask his team about the book drive," says Hi from the other end of the table. The girl beside him is showing him how to make a paper airplane.

"He wants you to ask them if some of the books can come here," adds Angel.

116

Officer Grant looks at Angel and Hi and then at Jomon. "Is this true?"

Jomon nods.

"All right," she says. "I'll ask."

She says her goodbyes and leaves the schoolroom.

"Can I have this?" asks Cora, holding up Jomon's card. "I can pretend it belongs to me."

Jomon takes the card from her, puts it back in the envelope, crosses out his name and writes Cora's name in its place.

He hands it back to her and says, "Now it really does belong to you."

20

"If you know something, you had better tell us," the chief executive says to Mrs. Simson. "We don't want to have to call the police."

They are all back in his office. He drags his desk chair out into the middle of the room and orders Mrs. Simson to sit down. He and the three other officials stand and look down at her.

The chief executive can never remember if it is more intimidating to make someone sit while he stands, or to make them stand while he sits. He suspects he's gotten it wrong this time. Mrs. Simson looks very comfortable in his high-backed, well-cushioned office chair.

"You wrote that note," accuses the security head. "Don't try to deny it."

"I signed my name to it," says Mrs. Simson. Aside from being angry, she is surprised how calm she feels. She is not afraid of these people.

"No, indeed," says the chief executive, wondering, as he talks, how he can get Mrs. Simson out of his chair. "We do not want to have to call the police. Here at the national museum we think of ourselves as family. We would prefer to keep this little incident a family secret. We hope you have not been gossiping about it."

"I think secrets are a problem," says Mrs. Simson. She speaks slowly, wanting to say the right words in the right order. She has been thinking deeply about this since Gather's disappearance. "We all need our privacy, of course, but that's totally different from keeping secrets. What secrets? All our secrets are the same! We get lonely, we get sad, other people hurt us, we hurt other people. Those are everybody's secrets! Why not talk about them? They might not seem quite as big if we talk about them."

In the quiet that follows her words, Mrs. Simson discovers that the chief executive's chair swivels as well as rocks. She has a good time swaying from side to side.

"My auntie always says, 'A problem shared is a problem half-solved,'" says the marketing manager.

"That's a good one," says the financial officer. "Mine says, 'Two heads are better than one.'"

"Unless one of those heads is a criminal," injects the security head. He's a bit miffed that this cleaner person is not intimidated by him. "Mrs. Simson, I think you are involved in this theft of property. Yes, I said theft! Are you trying to pad your cleaner's salary? Are you holding the sloth for ransom?"

Mrs. Simson goes on as if the security head hasn't spoken.

"I can't tell you how many people I've heard tell their secrets to Gather," she says. "Old, young, police officers, well-dressed people, poorly dressed people. They don't see me watching them. I'm just the cleaner. I can be mopping right beside them and they don't notice. They pour out their troubles. They sense Gather can carry them."

"What is she talking about?" asks the chief executive.

Mrs. Simson stops swiveling the chair. "Those same people who are showing their pain to a statue of a giant sloth will clam up and slap a smile on their face if a living person asks how they are." Mrs. Simson knows this because she has seen it and because she has done it herself. "Then they go away feeling worse, not better. They have a one-way conversation with something that can't respond to them any more than this metal desk."

As she speaks, Mrs. Simson admits to herself just how lonely she is.

I have to make changes, she thinks. *I cannot settle for this being my life.*

"Will someone please tell me what she is talking about?" the chief executive asks again.

"I don't have a clue," says the head of security from behind his dark glasses.

Mrs. Simson thinks about the giant sloth footprints in the dust. Gather has somehow come alive and gotten herself out into the world. Maybe she, Mrs. Simson, can get out into the world, too, and the first step is to find her friend and make sure she's all right.

Mrs. Simson reaches for the telephone and pushes it in the chief executive's direction.

"Call the police," she says. "You should have done that already. Right now. Call them."

"We don't answer to you," says the chief executive.

She decides to call the police herself.

"I need to report a disappearance," Mrs. Simson says into the phone. "No, not a theft. Not a missing person either, exactly … Runaway? Yes, I need to report a runaway. Who is in charge of runaways? Officer Olivia Grant? Then I would like to speak with her. She's out? Then please have her come to the national museum as soon as she gets back."

Mrs. Simson puts the receiver back in its place.

She cannot keep herself from smiling.

21

Lights out, and Jomon is on his cot in the dorm.

He slaps at a mosquito. He rolls over onto his side, then back onto his back.

It is way too early to be in bed.

Supper — a bread roll with peanut butter — was not that long ago. Then shower time, then half an hour of free time in the dorm room before the guard flicked off the light and told them, "Not a sound."

The moon is bright enough that the boys can continue to play under its light. Jomon sits up and looks around.

The smaller boys have stones from the yard that they have turned into cars. They are using the bed sheets to construct mountains and highways. Lucky and another one of the older boys grab the sheets, ball them up and toss them into a corner.

The smaller boys don't complain. They wait until the older boys have moved on, then retrieve the sheets and start again.

Jomon sees Angel playing a game of pickup sticks with a few other boys, using twigs they have collected from the yard. There are whispered arguments from that group.

"I saw it move!" "No, you didn't." "I saw it! My turn."

"Here's how it works," Lucky said to Jomon before lights out. "Someone makes a sound, the guard comes, someone goes to solitary. The guard doesn't care who. If it's me that goes, and you made the noise, you'd better be gone before I get out. You hear me?"

Jomon heard.

"Tell your brothers," said Lucky.

"They're not —" But Lucky had already moved on.

One of the boys has a deck of cards. The game they started before bedtime continues in a beam of light from the full moon.

Hi is in the middle of that group.

"Six of clubs," he whispers.

"That's a nine," says a boy. "Are you cheating?"

"Nine? Really?" asks Hi. "If you're so smart, why are you in here?"

"I killed a boy who was cheating at cards."

"No, you didn't," says a third boy. "You tried to sneak into the go-kart place."

"Hi's having a good time," says Angel, coming to sit on the foot of Jomon's bed. "I don't think he got much time to play when he was a kid."

"Nothing seems to bother him," says Jomon, sitting up. "Was he always like that?"

"I don't know," says Angel. "I got the drunk and sad Hi. I don't know what he was like before my mother died."

Jomon slaps at another mosquito. "Are you still mad at him?"

"I should be," says Angel. "I planned out a whole speech I'd say to him if I ever saw him again, about how he was a terrible father and just brought misery to my life."

"And now?"

"He's still all that, but I don't know what the point is in telling him. He won't get it. He's not like us."

"What do you mean?"

"He had his father with him all his life. He can't understand what it was like for me to not have him. I could give him my speech but then what? Probably nothing, and where would that leave me? No, I think I'll forget about the speech. I would like one thing, though."

"What's that?"

"I want him to call me Angel."

"You going to tell him that?"

Angel sighs. "What if I tell him and he still calls me Dev?"

"I think it's worth a try." Jomon looks over at the card players. They've stopped the game and are now trying to make a tower with the cards. Hi adds one to the tower. Everything collapses. Hi's smile is so broad it seems to take up his whole head.

"I think he likes to be liked," says Jomon. "I think he wants you to like him."

Angel thinks about it. "Maybe. What about you? It sounds like my grandson was a hard father to have. There must have been some good times, though?"

Jomon remembers his father shaping ends of lumber into shelves for Jomon's room. Jomon handing him the nails, the two of them smoothing down the wood with sandpaper. He remembers riding on his father's shoulders, high, high, high above the Mashramani parade, seeing all the costumes, smelling the food.

But there are other memories, too. His father's face near his, angry, drunk and spitting. Oozy, boozy vomit stinking on the floor. Knowing that anything Jomon and his mother did or did not do would be wrong.

"We had a big fight," Jomon says, "after Mum died. I didn't know how sick she was. I mean, she often had pain because my father hit her, but she pretended she didn't and I pretended to believe her. When she finally went to a doctor, it was too late. The cancer had spread from her pancreas to her liver and everywhere else. She was dead a week later."

"How did your dad handle that?"

"Same as he handled everything else. He drank. Mum's church lady friends showed up with a collection they'd taken to help with her funeral. He threw them out when they wouldn't hand over the money to him. He was falling-down drunk, so why would they trust him? As they left, one of them told me that they would see she was buried in her family plot near New Amsterdam. I never even knew she had a family plot."

"You never went to look for her grave?"

"I asked Dad about it after he'd sobered up a bit. He said I always did side with Mum and if I wanted to go, I should go, but then I could keep on going."

"And you were afraid to lose the last parent you had," says Angel.

"I let her down," says Jomon. "I'm ... nothing. I'm just nothing."

He turns away from Angel and curls up on his bunk.

"Hey, Jomon. Come to the window," whispers Hi. "You've got to see this! Angel — come on!"

Angel leaves the bed. Jomon hears excited whispering and the quiet pushing of kids. He puts his arms over his head. He wishes he could retreat to Jomonland. He wishes he had killed himself back in the police-station lockup.

"Jomon," says Angel. "You really ought to come here and see this."

But Jomon is done for the day. He stays on his cot, his eyes closed, and leaves the others to ooh and aah at whatever they are seeing out the window.

22

Gather knows she has an audience. She can smell them, boy humans and girl humans. They are keeping their distance, just watching her.

If they attack, she knows how to disappear into the forest.

She gives most of her attention to one of her favorite activities — eating!

The land she once knew as home has changed in many ways, but Guyana is still a garden. Gather has eaten her way from the museum to the detention center, following her nose and the tree line, getting ever closer to the haven of the rainforest.

She is in no hurry. No one is chasing her. Most humans ignore her. The young ones point at her but are pulled along by the grown-ups, who are always in a hurry. The old ones see her and nod.

She stretches to the full height of her reach to snag a choice clump of flowers in her claws. She hears a "Whoa!" sound from the young humans, but it is a sound of admiration.

She pulls down the flowers, dislodging a huge seed pod that crashes to the ground and explodes with a boom.

The young humans cheer quietly. Gather eats and eats and eats until her generous belly is full, for now.

She goes to sleep in the thicket just as the sun gets ready to start another day.

23

The next morning, Jomon watches others kick a ball around the yard. He's leaning against a wall, out of the way of the game.

Cora runs up to him.

"I made this for you," she says.

She holds out a white tissue-paper flower.

"Put it away," she says. "I don't want anyone to laugh at me."

He puts it in his trouser pocket — the pocket that once held his geography medal.

"You're not my boyfriend!" Cora says quickly. Then she darts away like a rabbit.

Jomon wants to laugh. Then he wants to cry.

The world is garbage, he thinks. *Nobody wants that kid? The world is garbage.* He will be well rid of it.

After lunch and chores, the teacher declares an art period. The young prisoners draw with bits of crayon while the teacher reads to them from *A Christmas Carol*.

Jomon doesn't feel like drawing. He doesn't feel like doing anything. Angel gets up from his chair, squeezes past other prisoners to Jomon, picks up a random crayon and places it in Jomon's hand. When Jomon still doesn't do anything, Hi comes over and moves Jomon's crayon hand on the paper.

"Draw," says Hi.

The teacher keeps reading.

Jomon looks at the line Hi has made him draw, a dark purple crayon mark. He draws another line to add to it, then another, then another.

Half an hour later, when Jomon's paper is filled with purple marks, Officer Grant walks back into the schoolroom, carrying a cardboard box.

"Come and see what we have for you today!"

The young prisoners gather around.

Jomon stays put. He sees the name of his old school on the box and he knows what is inside it. His classmates came through.

The young prisoners lift the donated books out of the box one by one and spread them out all over the table. Books on stars, animals, sports and fish. Books of poetry, history, heroes and stories, books with big pictures and small words and books with no pictures and big words.

Officer Grant stacks the artwork into a pile to make more room for the books. She glances down at the drawing at the top of the pile, then holds it up to look at it more closely. She looks at the next one, and the one after that. She sifts through the stack of drawings, looking from one to the other. She leans beside Jomon and examines the art more closely.

Jomon sees the drawings are all of the same thing: a giant, hairy creature eating the flowers off cannonball trees.

"Yours is different," Officer Grant says to Jomon.

In dark purple, Jomon has drawn his mother's face.

Her chin is a little bit pointy, just like his own. The dimple in her left cheek. Her eyes, kind, amused, concerned.

How are things in Jomonland?

"Is that your mother?" Officer Grant picks up the drawing, looks at it for a moment, then puts it back on the table. She gives Jomon's shoulder a quick squeeze.

"Officer Grant, where did all these books come from?" one of the young prisoners asks.

Jomon looks up and catches her eye. He gives his head a little shake.

"I believe the name of the school is on the box," Officer Grant says, leaving Jomon's side. "Why don't you see if you can find it?"

"Here it is!" says Cora. "Durban Park Community High School."

"Excellent," says the teacher. "We have a place where we can send our thank-you letters."

"Can I write my letter on the back of my drawing?"

Officer Grant puts the drawings back on the table so the letters can be written. To Jomon, she says, "I've thought about getting books for this place for a long time, but other things always get in the way. This is a good thing you did. I won't forget it."

———

Later, Jomon heads back to the dorm with the other boys to wait for supper. He stretches out on his cot and looks at the drawing of his mother's face. He places it face down against his chest.

He looks around the dorm. Boys are reading. A few read silently to themselves. Two share a copy of a Black Panther graphic novel. Angel sits with one of the smaller boys and reads out loud from *My Side of the Mountain*. Hi is sitting on the end of Lucky's cot, while Lucky reads to him from *A Treasury of Animal Stories*.

Jomon gets up and walks to the window. He wishes he could tell his mother about the books. It was the sort of thing she was always doing — cooking for sick neighbors, collecting clothes for a family who'd lost their home in a fire.

She would be proud of him for the books.

He is pulled from his thoughts by the sight of Officer Grant walking around the cannonball trees. He watches as she looks around and shades her eyes to see better. She takes a step, then lifts up her foot as if she has stepped in something unpleasant. She takes a plastic evidence bag out of her pocket and collects a sample from the ground.

Jomon wonders what in the world she is doing.

24

"There may have been sightings."

Officer Grant is meeting with the museum officials in the chief executive's office later that night. Mrs. Simson is with them.

"There *may* have been sightings?" the security head asks. "What does that mean?"

"It means there may have been sightings," says Officer Grant. She keeps a close eye on the officials while she talks.

Her specialty on the police force is looking for child runaways. Finding the runaway is only half the work. The other part is finding out why the child ran. More than one hitting parent has come under Officer Grant's critical eye.

"Where were these sightings?" the chief executive asks. "We'll get a team over there now and retrieve it."

"This is now a police matter," says Officer Grant. "You'll do nothing without our say so."

"Excuse me," says the head of security, sounding not at all like he feels he needs to be excused, "but the sloth is our property. If you know where it is, you have to give it back to us."

"If it is stolen property, it must be held as evidence," says Officer Grant. "If it is lost property, then we must do an investigation to see who is responsible for such an expensive loss. And if it is a runaway, then I will need to determine why the sloth ran away and what is the best place for it to live in from now on."

"It's a museum exhibit," says the chief executive. "Museum exhibits don't run away."

Officer Grant keeps secret from the officials something she has in her pocket — an analysis of the dung sample she collected after stepping in it in the cannonball thicket. The zoologist at the Georgetown zoo says it's from the sloth family, but not from any sloth she's ever seen.

"She is not an 'it'," says Mrs. Simson. "Her name is Gather. And she wasn't stolen or lost. She walked away. I showed you the footprints."

"She," agrees Officer Grant, nodding at Mrs. Simson. "We'll be looking into all possibilities. Now, what sort of habitat would Gather prefer?"

The officials look at their shoes.

Finally, the marketing manager says, "Giant ground sloths have been extinct for twenty thousand years."

"Ten thousand," corrects Mrs. Simson.

"Extinct or not, what terrain would she head for? Jungle? Shore? Open fields?"

None of the officials knows.

"I deal with finances," says the financial officer.

"I find ways to bring people into the museum," says the marketing manager.

"I have lunch with funders," says the chief executive.

"And I protect everyone and everything," says the head of security.

Officer Grant shakes her head. "You mean to tell me that you are around these amazing exhibits every day — a privilege not many people in Guyana have — and you haven't taken the time to learn about them? I should arrest you all for laziness."

"Gather will go to the forest," Mrs. Simson says. "Megatherium can stand on their hind legs, reaching up into the trees to eat leaves and flowers and fruit. She'll need food and she'll need places where she can get away from people. If she can get to a forest, that's where she'll be the most happy."

"Someone here knows a thing or two," says Officer Grant. "I've never had to look for a runaway prehistoric ground sloth before. I'm going to need expert help."

She turns to Mrs. Simson. "How would you like to be my deputy on this?"

Mrs. Simson does not need to be asked twice. She takes the supply cupboard key out of her uniform pocket and hands it to the chief executive.

"But you're the cleaner!" he says.

"The broom is in the closet," Mrs. Simson says. And, just like Gather, she walks out of the museum.

25

"Jomon. Jomon, wake up."

Jomon is pulled from the sleep he finally fell into. Hi is shaking his leg and Angel is standing beside the bed.

"Get up," whispers Angel. "You're coming with us."

"Where?"

"You're going to say goodbye to your mother," says Hi.

"It's the one thing you want to do, and we're going to help you do it," says Angel.

"Leave me alone." Jomon realizes that he is gripping the white paper flower Cora gave him. He drops it to the floor. Angel picks it up and puts it back in Jomon's hand.

"Guard Boyton has a sick child at home," Angel says. "She left the dorm door unlocked."

"They'll catch us in the yard and I'll be back in solitary," Jomon says.

"Maybe," says Hi. "Maybe not. Maybe you'll think of something once we get into the yard."

"Leave me alone," Jomon says again.

"Look," says Hi, sitting down on the bed. "You're planning on killing yourself anyway. Why not come with us? What, really, have you got to lose?"

Jomon looks from Hi to Angel. Then he swings his feet to the floor.

The three boys grab their sandals and head to the door. They open it and step out. They move soundlessly down the steps and into the yard.

The main gate is closed and locked. The boys are faced with a high fence topped with strands of barbed wire.

Not knowing how he knows to do this, Jomon picks up the Welcome mat and tosses it up to the top of the fence. It straddles the barbed wire. In seconds, he is up and over and on the other side.

"Go ahead, son," Hi says to Angel. "I'll watch out for you."

Jomon sees Angel smile. Then Angel climbs and jumps and joins Jomon on the other side.

Hi is last. After he climbs over the barbed wire, he pulls the Welcome mat off the pointed barbs and tosses it back down to the office door. It lands on the stoop, silently and perfectly straight, not a speck of dirt on it.

THE GREATS

The air smells sweeter on the free side of the fence.

Jomon and the great-grandfathers head to the cover of the cannonball trees. At the very last second, Jomon swerves, narrowly escaping stepping in the largest single pile of dung he has ever seen.

The young humans walk within feet of Gather, but they don't notice her. She is very good at blending in with her surroundings.

She has eaten every cannonball flower she can reach in the grove. She has had a little nap, and she's thinking of moving on. This is a nice spot that she's in, but there's a bit too much human noise and too few trees.

She watches the young humans head down the road. As humans go, they seem harmless.

She strolls off in the same direction, keeping a good distance, staying sheltered by the trees. She lets out a giant burp from all the cannonball flowers. It goes out into the night as just another forest sound.

When there are no trees to shelter her, she hurries across the open area, doing the rolling walk on the outside of her feet, protecting her long claws on the ends of her toes.

Gather's belly is full, she is protected by the darkness and she is free to be curious.

Really, she is just free.

26

Jomon feels free. He feels like a baby goat, ready to kick and jump in a field.

He starts running and the others run with him. They move their legs and swing their arms, push air in and out of their lungs and crank their hearts up as fast as they'll pump.

Jomon, Angel and Hi run until they can't run another step, and then they walk — not talking, just enjoying the rhythm of one foot in front of the other.

Jomon has never been out in this type of darkness, away from streetlights, with the stars looking so bright and so close he can almost jump and bump them with his head. He has never been on a long walk like this before. He is surprised to realize that he is actually enjoying himself, moving through his country with his two feet and his heartbeat.

Days can get hot in Guyana, even with the lovely winds coming in from the sea. The boys walk on the open road as long as they can, but as morning brightens the sky, they shift to pathways through the bush that run parallel to the road. From here they can more easily duck and cover if they see the police.

This path is safer, but it also traps the air and super heats it with humidity from the plants.

In the middle of the day, Hi makes them stop.

"We need to rest," he tells Jomon. "We need food and water."

Jomon knows Hi is right but he doesn't know what to do about it. Where are they going to sleep? What are they going to eat? He has no money.

"The land will feed us," Hi says. He leads them off the path to a secluded spot by a pond. There is shade and a large mossy boulder nearby to give them privacy.

The boys sweep the ground with their feet to scare away any snakes. Then they stretch out. The boulder is covered with a strange, bristly moss, and it feels warm and soft. Everyone dozes off.

Some time later, Jomon wakes with a start. The highest heat of the day has passed. The afternoon is thinking about slowly meandering into evening.

Hi has a small fire burning. He's caught three little fish and has them roasting on sticks over coals. Also in the coals are coconut half-shells full of boiled water.

"This one's cooled a bit," says Angel, holding a shell full of water out to Jomon. "Don't gulp it, though. It's still hot."

Jomon sips and feels the water flood into his cells. It is the best drink of water he has ever had.

"Fish is almost ready," says Hi.

Jomon spots a mango tree and picks three ripe mangoes to add to their meal.

The three boys sit around the fire. Hi hands a big leaf full of roasted fish to Jomon and another one to Angel.

Jomon alternates fingers full of crispy fish with bites of sweet mango. Juice runs down his chin.

It all tastes so good! He's eaten only awful jail food for days. His mother taught him how to cook a little bit when she was alive, but he never really paid attention. Why had he never thought to cook food over a fire? He could learn how to cook good meals. Then he and Dad could sit around the fire and eat and —

"Dev, eat your fish."

Jomon notices that Angel hasn't touched his food.

"Dev!" orders Hi. "I cooked that for you. Eat it!"

Angel picks up the leaf with the roasted fish on it and hands it to Jomon. He gets up from the fire and walks away.

"I did the best I could for you, Dev Fowler," Hi calls after him. "There's no pleasing you. What more could I do?"

"You could call him by his name," says Jomon.

"His name?" Hi repeats. "Everyone calls him Dev. Everyone laughs about it!"

"Just because everyone laughs doesn't make it funny," says Angel.

Father and son glare at each other. Hi is the first to soften his face.

"That's just what your mother would have said," Hi says thoughtfully.

He stands up, takes the leaf full of fish from Jomon and holds it out to Angel.

"We've got a long way to go," he says. "Better eat up ... Angel."

Angel's shoulders relax. He eats the fish. They put out the fire and head back out on their journey — walking, walking, walking.

27

Jomon and the great-grandfathers walk along quiet stretches where Jomon can almost hear the sea. They walk through villages busy with buying and selling and families hurrying between home, work and school. They walk along pathways with people on bicycles, goats chewing on weeds, and past homes where old people sit on the porches and watch the world go by.

"Three boys, just what I need," says an elderly woman at a roadside stand called True Love. Bob Marley is playing over a speaker. "Put these crates in the back for me, would you, and take the old ones out. They're coming to pick up the empties tomorrow, and my back isn't as strong as it used to be."

Jomon, Hi and Angel lift and carry and sweat for almost an hour while the woman sits on a bench under the shop's awning, fanning herself and making comments like, "Pick up your feet, I've got customers coming," and "The Lord sent you boys to me so there must be some good in you," which makes Jomon wonder why they are bothering to work so hard.

But when the job is finished, she brings them plates of the best chicken curry and rice Jomon has ever tasted, and cold bottles of soda to wash it down.

While they eat, she tells them the story of her family, which she has traced all the way back to Mali.

"Got a daughter now who works at the national zoo," she says. "In charge of the ocelots. Always was wild about cats."

Customers start to gather as the boys finish eating. They return their plates, thank the woman and head back to the road.

The sun sets and the moon rises. The darkness of the night mixed with the sudden brightness of car headlights or bare lightbulbs over a shop keep Jomon's eyes adjusting to no light and then too much light. People seem to appear out of nowhere, slipping into his field of vision, then slipping back out of it as he, Hi and Angel walk in and out of shadows.

Jomon enjoys the challenge of it, the way he has to watch out for dogs and children and donkey carts and trucks. It takes all of his concentration.

The villages come to an end for a time and the boys walk on in darkness.

Jomon has never walked this much, and he is a little surprised that he can do it. His legs are tired and his feet are still a little sore from the cuts, but it's nothing he can't tolerate.

Guyana is a small country. Jomon thinks back to the maps he studied for the geography competition. Other than a few boat rides across the Demerara and Essequibo Rivers, he could probably cover the whole country on foot, from Corriverton by the Suriname border to Waini Point by Venezuela, and then south to where the Rupununi savannah meets the Kamoa Mountains and Brazil. He could get to know his country through his feet and through the people he'd meet. He could learn everyone's language — all the Amerindian languages and the languages people brought with them from their old home countries. He could try all the foods, sing all the songs, and listen to all the stories.

"You can't do any of that if you kill yourself," says Angel. "It's an obvious point, but one worth mentioning."

"I like his idea," says Hi. "Walk, walk, walk. If you don't like where you are, walk to someplace else."

"It's just an idea," says Jomon. "Just a daydream. It wouldn't fix anything."

He imagines himself walking, walking, walking with the heavy emptiness always in his head. He wouldn't ever be able to really see anything, taste anything or appreciate anything.

"You mean it wouldn't fix everything," says Angel. "No one thing fixes everything."

"Then why the hell didn't *you* do it?" Jomon asks them.

Hi and Angel have nothing to say for a long time.

Then Hi asks Angel, "Instead of killing myself, would you rather I'd just walked away?"

"You were always walking away from me," says Angel. "What was so horrible about me? What was so horrible that you had to kill yourself to get away from me? I was just a kid!"

Angel is not quite shouting, but his voice is rising. Jomon sees a couple of houses just off the highway and doesn't want anybody waking up and calling the police on them.

"Let's keep moving," he whispers.

Dawn breaks. They walk through another village.

Just as they reach its outskirts, the sky opens up. Sudden, hard rains are a Guyana staple.

The boys jump over a gully and dash into a Rotary playground. They head for a little playhouse built over a monkey bars and swing set. They rush into the playhouse and plop down on the floor, rain streaming down their faces.

They look from one to another in the dim light. Hi starts laughing.

"You two look like something that came out of the swamp!"

Jomon and Angel laugh, too.

"We're the creatures from the black lagoon," says Jomon.

"Did you see that movie, too?" asks Angel. "I love that movie."

"What's a movie?" asks Hi.

Jomon and Angel tell him, shouting to be heard over the torrent of rain on the playhouse roof. They explain plots, mimic their favorite characters and sing bits of their favorite movie songs.

The rain stops as suddenly as it starts. As the boys unfold themselves to leave the playhouse, a new sound reaches them.

It is rhythmic clapping — jazzy and fun. Jomon and the grandfathers leave the playhouse and stand on the bridge of the playset.

A boy is coming toward them from across the park. He is about their size. He is clapping and dancing and stomping his feet in the puddles to the beat of his hands.

Closer and closer, the dancing fellow grooves his way to the playground. He looks like he is having a great time.

The boy dances closer.

150

Angel takes a quick, hard breath. Tears are rolling down his cheeks.

The boy gets even closer. He is singing. Jomon can make out the words. The boy is singing them brightly, not slowly, turning them into a celebration instead of a lullaby.

> *Chatter monkeys in the trees*
> *Swaying branches in the breeze*
> *Sleep the hours of dark away*
> *Wake up to a brighter day.*

With a graceful twirl, the boy leaps up on the play structure and grabs hold of the bridge bar, swinging up to Jomon and the grandfathers.

"I am Barnabus Bangla Fowler," he says. "Stage name — Barnby. Which one of you is my grandson?"

28

Angel bursts into sobs.

Jomon and Hi get him off the play structure. He drops to his knees.

"I'm sorry," Angel cries. "I'm so sorry."

"Pops, Pops, no," says Barnby, kneeling beside him. "It's all right. Don't cry! I can't stand to see you sad."

"I let you down."

"Pops, this is a happy day. It's so good to see you. I need you to be happy to see me. Damn it, why can't you ever be happy?"

Barnby turns his back on his father and stomps away. He turns around after a few steps and shouts over his shoulder.

"Well, come on!"

Jomon helps Angel to his feet. Barnby slows down so they can catch up, but his back is stiff.

They walk through one village, then the next. They reach the mouth of the Berbice River and rest on its shaded bank.

Finally, Angel speaks.

"I *am* happy," he says to Barnby. "I am really, really happy to see you."

"Then show me," Barnby says. "Show me that you feel more than just misery about things you think you've done."

"I do!" says Angel.

"No, you don't," says Barnby. "But right now, I'm here for Jomon."

"We're all here for Jomon," says Hi.

"You're my grandfather?" Barnby asks Hi.

Hi grins and holds out his hand. Barnby doesn't take it.

"You're the reason my pops is the way he is. Well, part of the reason. So, thanks a lot."

"Who are you to talk to me that way?" Hi demands. "Who do you think you are? You don't even know me."

"And whose fault is that?" asks Barnby. "You decided to take yourself out of my father's life, and that made him so sad, he took himself out of mine."

Angel drops to the ground and hides his face in his hands. Hi and Barnby stand over him, chests puffed out, feet planted, arms tight. They glare at each other.

"You can't blame his suicide on me!" Hi shouts. "I wasn't even there!"

"That's right," Barnby yells back. "You weren't there."

"How'd you do with *your* son?" Hi snarls at Barnby. "How good a father were you?"

Barnby flies at Hi and Hi flies at Barnby and the pair of them hit the dirt.

Jomon walks away. He's done with all of them. They are just ignorant kids, not wise men or ghosts from another world.

Jomon is on his own.

His mother's grave is somewhere on the west bank of the Berbice River. He is going to find where she is buried, tell her goodbye, then put this whole damn life behind him.

He walks and walks and walks, leaving the fighting and crying behind.

The rhythm of the walk calms him. There is something soothing about his feet hitting the ground, one in front of the other, again and again and again. He has no one to bug him, the sky is blue above, and the world is spread out in front of him.

He sees a church steeple and heads for it. Next to the church is a cemetery.

"Wait!"

Jomon turns around. The new boy, Barnby, runs up to him.

"She's not there."

"I'll check it out for myself," says Jomon. "By myself."

"I'll go with you," says Barnby.

"By myself means without you."

"You are never without me," Barnby says. "You're never without any of us."

Jomon walks on his own through the cemetery, looking at all the grave markers, searching for his mother's name. He goes through the whole cemetery.

His mother is not here.

"I know where she is," says Barnby. He is leaning against a tall headstone with the other two grandfathers. They seem to have declared a truce.

"So tell me," says Jomon.

"I'll take you there," says Barnby. "And on the way, I'll tell you my story."

29

Grandfather's Contribution

My best memories are of making Pops and Ma laugh.

You wouldn't think there would be anything to laugh about in a leprosy hospital, but there was always something — and it was usually me!

The home for kids who didn't have leprosy was outside the hospital fence. It was run by nuns. So was the home inside the fence, but that was for the children who had leprosy. I snuck in there a lot. The first big routine I did, when I actually thought about it and planned it out in advance, was for the kids in that home.

Here's what I did. I helped out in the laundry, because I always liked my clothes to be just so, even though they were charity clothes. Especially since they were charity clothes, which were little more than rags.

My father used to bring me new clothes, but I shared them around. It didn't seem right to be wearing nice new things when no one else was. Most of the kids had no one to bring them stuff. When someone in the family has leprosy, it's like the whole family has leprosy. Friends don't stick around, and relatives forget they know you. My pops was one of the only fathers who ever came to visit.

I remember the day he saw a shirt he gave me on some other kid.

"That's my son's shirt," he complained to Sister Carolyn. "Why is my son's shirt on that boy's back?"

The boy — his name was Owen — shrank into himself. I watched it happen. He'd been so happy to see my pops because Pops was an actual father. Not Owen's father, but still, a father.

I'm off track already.

I helped out in the laundry and that meant I had access to the nuns' habits. This was in the full wimple days, before Vatican II, all gowns and long veils.

I borrowed a habit, put it on and snuck into the children's ward inside the fence. I hid around a corner until the nuns on duty left the ward for Mass, then I popped into the room and pretended to take a little boy's pulse. At first he just stared at me in shock, but then he burst out laughing. All the kids did. It was terrific. I tripped over the hem of the habit, balanced a chamber pot — empty — on my head, did some sort of dance. All silly, but the audience loved it.

I heard the nuns coming back and ran off before they caught me. I went to my mother's ward and did a repeat performance there. Everyone loved it. Even the nuns, although they tried to hide it.

Over the years, I developed the nun routine more and more, and when I grew up, it became a big hit in my act. I became Sister Barnby, a bit dotty but always the smartest person in the room, never afraid to put anyone in their place, especially the pompous. It always got laughs, but it was never mean or disrespectful. Those nuns took good care of us, and I never wanted to make them look bad.

Ma just loved me. I could make her laugh or not. I could sit on her bed and do my schoolwork or just doze next to her on the cot until the nursing sister kicked me out.

It was different with Pops. He was always so sad when he came to see me. I couldn't tell him I missed him or that one of the boys in the dorm kept hiding my toothbrush or that I wanted him to find a job close to the hospital so I could live with him and still see Ma every day. I couldn't say anything that might make him sadder, so I was always smiling, always joking. Sometimes, if I said or did something really funny, I could get him to smile all the way up to his eyes, but only for a few seconds. I just wanted to see him happy.

Mostly, Pops wasn't there. My life was the children's home, sneaking into the hospital cottages to see Ma and the kids with leprosy and coming up with new ways to make people laugh.

It was all about comedy until the day it became more than that. Visiting hours were over in the hospital and all the kids were being rounded up to go back to the other side of the fence, the non-leprosy side. I wasn't ready to leave Ma, so I just pretended to leave, then doubled back and ducked under the bed.

The medical staff did their rounds. They came to my mother's bed. In those days they treated leprosy with injections of chaulmoogra nut oil. The injections hurt. I heard my mother cry out. Then they changed the dressing on an ulcer that had opened up on her ankle. That hurt her, too.

I'd never heard her cry before. I realized then that she was always being cheerful for me, just like I was always being cheerful for Pops.

When I first heard her cry, I rolled into a ball and put my hands over my ears. Then I unrolled, crawled out from under the bed, sat beside her and put my hand on her shoulder.

I sang her the Soothing Song — the song Pops sang for me when I was small and skinned my knee or had a bad dream, back before we moved to the hospital.

I sang the song over and over. Some of the other women in the ward picked it up and sang it with me.

The lines in my mother's face softened. I could feel her let go of the tension the pain gave her. I'm not saying my voice had magic powers or anything, but it gave her something else to focus on, something good. Jokes are good, but they weren't right for that moment.

I decided right then that I would learn to entertain people in a lot of different ways, so I could give them what they needed when they needed it.

Letting Ma know that I could see her pain and not run away from it meant that she didn't have to pretend with me anymore. We could talk about things, really talk. I think that she thought her son might have some good stuff inside him. At least, I like to think that.

I wish I had done that with Pops. If he had known I could see his sadness and that I loved him anyway, maybe that would have made things easier for him. He wouldn't have felt he had to bring gifts every time he came to see me, and I wouldn't have felt I had to have new jokes ready to make him laugh. We could have just been together.

160

Back to the story.

I asked Sister Carolyn if I could join the nuns' choir because I wanted to learn about music. She said no, but she created a new choir out of all the old-enough kids in the children's homes. We sang hymns and Christmas carols and put on a concert to raise money for the hospital. We raised enough to buy new sheets and pillows for every bed! Sister Carolyn taught me how to read music, play the piano and — secretly, because this was against the rules — she taught me how to tap dance. She'd been a chorus girl on Broadway before she became a nun!

Pops came to one of our concerts. He told me afterwards that he liked it and he was proud of me.

I loved him for that, but I wished he'd made more of an effort more often. What was wrong with me that I wasn't worth his effort? I gave him my effort all the time!

Ma died of pneumonia when I was thirteen. I left the hospital that had been my home. I left the nuns and the patients and the way of life I was used to. And I moved in with my father in Georgetown.

We didn't talk much. He didn't seem to know how. He always made sure I had food and clothes and money for school things, but we were like guests living in someone else's house.

School was hard at first when the kids found out that I'd lived at the leprosy hospital. Some of them made fun of me by saying, "Unclean! Unclean!" like in the Bible. One boy held up his arm with the hand tucked up inside the sleeve, like it had been eaten away by leprosy. Mean, ignorant stuff.

So I did something mean and ignorant back. I said, "Man, the world wishes you had leprosy. Anything would improve your ugly face!"

The boy's friends laughed, but I felt bad right away. Leprosy isn't a joke. Then I told them about all the people I knew at the hospital, their names, where they were from, what they were like. And then I started in on the nuns. I turned into Sister Barnby. They laughed. I got invited to join the school drama club. I became almost popular.

Things were going along okay. I got busy with my own life and so I didn't notice Pop's sadness as much.

And then, in my last year of high school, everything fell apart.

We were in rehearsals for *Measure for Measure*. One of the other actors asked me to stay after to help him with his lines. We were running lines backstage when he leaned over and kissed me. And I kissed him back. And someone saw. And told.

I was expelled. The other boy couldn't be expelled because he was the principal's son, but I think I was the lucky one because that principal was an ass, and I can only imagine the hell that kid lived in.

My father was told why I was kicked out of school. He never said a word to me about it. His face was sad, but his face was always sad. I guessed that now he was sad to have me for his son.

Three days after I was kicked out of school, my father told me that a cousin of a man he worked with was willing to rent me part of his flat in New York City. Pops found me a job as a dish washer on a cargo ship that would take me to New York and pay me a bit of a wage at the same time. I left Guyana a week later. Pops took me to the docks. He handed me an envelope full of money. I was so ashamed I could barely even say goodbye.

The work on the ship was hard, but being on the ocean was terrific, and coming into New York was amazing. I thought Georgetown was a big city, but New York? Incredible.

Anyway, I managed to find the apartment and was greeted with the news that Angel, my father, was dead. He had killed himself. I had just turned eighteen years old.

Soon after he died, I got a large bank draft in the mail. Pops made sure to take care of his affairs before he killed himself so that I'd have enough money to keep going until I could pay my own way. I appreciated the money. I stretched it out on food and rent and bus fare and acting lessons. Every time I handed over a dollar, I wished I could have called Pops to tell him what I was doing.

I did all right. I got a job as a night cleaner in a big hospital. I went on lots of auditions. Got lots of rejections, but I did land the occasional job. One of the first jobs I got was because I'd gone in early for my shift at the hospital to entertain some of the patients before I had to get down to cleaning. One of the patients had a nephew who worked in an off-off-Broadway theater and got me a small part in their musical revue. Once I'd smoothed out my Guyana accent so Americans could understand me better, I booked more jobs.

I did a series of television commercials for a fruit company. I had to dance around with a basket of fruit on my head, a man version of Carmen Miranda. In one commercial, I popped up in a grocery store where ladies were trying to decide what to buy. In another, I popped up in a white lady's kitchen when she was trying to decide what to feed her kids for a snack. I was paid well for those jobs.

There were marches and rallies all the time in those days, for civil rights, to stop the war in Vietnam, to end poverty. Some of these rallies would have entertainment to help people feel good about what they were doing. Sometimes I'd take the stage as Sister Barnby and do a quick bit about going to the White House to give Richard Nixon a piece of my mind. Often, I sang backup for the headliners. I got to be on the same stage as Dick Gregory and Joan Baez. It was quite a time.

I never forgot that kiss in high school, trouble though it caused me, and in New York City I found out I wasn't alone. I met more people like me — men who liked men and women who liked women. There were clubs we could go to where no one would bother us. One was called the Stonewall Inn. I went there a lot. I was there the night the police raided it and the riots started. I was one of the people arrested. After some nights in jail, I got deported back to Guyana.

My career was over. Everything was over.

There wasn't much paying work for an actor in Georgetown, so I took a job at one of the newspapers, writing obituaries and ads. I ran into a girl I'd known in high school. We'd been in the drama club together. She was a teacher now. I got work at a radio station. I decided to marry this girl — your grandmother. We had a son together — your father — and stayed married for quite a few years until she told me she would rather live alone. She said she knew I was gay. She said that was all right with her, she wasn't put on this earth to judge. But she said if she was going to be lonely in a marriage, she'd rather just live alone with our son and have some breathing room around her.

I moved out. I became like my father and like his father — a part-time father. I could see clearly the road I was on. I was determined to stick it out until my son was raised.

I lasted until he was twenty-five.

Then I'd had enough. I was lonely. It was against the law to be gay in Guyana, so I had no companion and no hope of ever finding one. I was just alone.

So, I killed myself.

The moment I did it, I wished I hadn't.

But by then, I was dead.

It was too late to change my mind.

30

Jomon and the three grandfathers sit in the twisted roots of a cottonwood tree.

"We've all told you our stories," Hi says. "What have you decided?"

"What have I decided about what?"

"Are you still planning on killing yourself?"

Jomon looks from one boy to the other. He can see bits of his own face in each of their faces.

"You all did," he says. "You all got to go. Why shouldn't I?"

"We told you we regretted it," says Angel.

"I don't believe you." Jomon looks at Hi. "If you'd stayed alive, would you have changed your life, or just been the same miserable man, drinking and hurting everyone around you? Would you have taken the time to get to know your son? I think you killed yourself because you were too lazy to try to have a real conversation with the only person who really cared anything about you."

"No, no. I killed myself because I wanted to be with my wife."

"That's a lie," snaps Jomon. "You believe it because drunks believe their own lies. If you wanted to be with your wife, you'd do the things she liked to do. You said she liked to look at new things? You could have spent your own life looking at new things, starting with your son. She would have been with you then."

Jomon thinks of the things his mother loved. She loved to sit and draw with him at the kitchen table, using his crayons to create beautiful pictures of the Guyana countryside. She loved to sit on the front porch under a full moon, letting the moonbeams wash over her face. "Moonbathing," she called it.

He hasn't done either of those things since she died.

He turns to Angel. "I don't believe you, either, because if you'd stayed alive, you would have had to live with everyone knowing you had a gay son. You got him out of the country and set up for a new life, but do you really think that made up for him knowing you were ashamed of him?"

"I was not ashamed," Angel says to Barnby, who is

looking at the ground. "I was afraid for you. That's why I got you out."

"That explains why you sent him away," says Jomon. "That doesn't explain why you killed yourself instead of going away with him. You were prepared to end your life but you weren't prepared to change it? You could have been happy."

"I didn't think I deserved to be happy," says Angel. "My father never wanted me."

"So what?" asks Jomon. "Your son wanted you! I think you never wanted to be happy because then you'd have to admit that you wasted most of your life being miserable."

"No, no, I ..."

But Jomon has already moved on to Barnby.

"I understand you the least of all. You had way more opportunities than either of these two. You knew you had talent. I know you were lonely, but there are a lot of lonely people in Guyana. You could have helped them. Imagine what my father ..."

Jomon feels himself starting to cry. He shakes it off and gets to his feet.

"You're all liars and cowards," he yells. "You have nothing to teach me."

Nearby, in a small clump of trees, Gather is getting alarmed at the rising sound of the human voices.

Humans shouting often led to humans killing, and she does not want to be killed again.

The boy doing most of the shouting is coming closer and closer to Gather, getting louder and louder with each step. Gather peers down at him through the tree branches.

"I'm better than all of you because I'm going to kill myself *before* I have kids. You're the first suicide?" he asks Hi. "Well, I'm going to be the last. The whole sorry family ends with me."

The three other humans are now on their feet, moving quickly toward the shouting boy and Gather's hiding place.

She feels trapped. She needs to move. Plus, she smells a large stand of cannonball flowers on the other side of a big open area — an area, she can see from her great height, that is covered with humans.

There is a battle between her fear and her stomach. Her stomach is winning. She gets ready to move.

"You don't have to end the family pain by dying," shouts Angel. "You can end it by living."

"What's the point?" Jomon yells back. "You can't tell me it's not all lousy."

"You are so stubborn," says Barnby. "You're just like your father."

Jomon runs at Barnby and lands a punch, right to Barnby's head. Barnby drops to the ground.

"I *am* just like my father!" Jomon shouts. "He saw nothing good in this world, and neither do I! You are all just empty, useless ghosts. Tell me one thing worth living for. Just one thing. You can't! Because there is nothing! It's all garbage. It's all —"

Gather steps out of the thicket, right in front of Jomon.

First comes one giant, hairy leg, a leg as tall as a person and as thick as a tree, with a foot as big as a boat and toenails long and curvy.

Out swings her other leg, then her tummy, round like the moon. Then her arms ending in claws that can get her any fruit or flower she desires.

Jomon looks up, way up. Then up some more.

The words he was going to say vanish from his throat. All thoughts are forgotten as Jomon stares up at Gather. The three grandfathers stand by his side.

Jomon has been to the museum. He knows what he is looking at.

"It's Megatherium," he breathes. "But they're supposed to be extinct."

"So are we, my great-great-grandson," says Hi. "So are we."

31

Mrs. Simson is having the time of her life.

She is zooming around Guyana in a police car, talking with people about missing boys and a missing sloth, seeing places she has never dreamed of seeing.

Her life up to this point has been cleaning at the museum and going to church. She has cleaning clothes and church clothes

Today, she is wearing her cleaning clothes.

When all this is over, she thinks, *I'm going to buy some adventure clothes.*

"Oh, my goodness," says Officer Grant.

A small crowd fills the road in front of them. Rising far above it is the top of a creature that hasn't walked the earth in ten thousand years.

Mrs. Simson leaps from the police car before it

comes to a complete stop. She pushes her way through the crowd with the ease of an eel slipping through seagrass.

"Make way," she says, her voice resonating with absolute authority. "Special deputy in charge of animal antiquities, coming through."

The crowd doesn't fight her. People push each other gently to get a better view, but no one shouts or throws things. Some raise up their smartphones and cameras to take pictures. Others lift their children to their shoulders so they can see.

Mrs. Simson moves through the crowd and then she is with Gather.

Looking like the Queen of the Continent, the giant ground sloth is surrounded by four teen boys — two in the front and two in the back — and a growing crowd of admirers.

Angel and Barnby walk behind Gather. Her caiman-sized tail sways from side to side. Sometimes the boys manage to jump out of the way. Sometimes, it knocks them down. When Angel gets knocked down, he laughs and laughs, then gets up to get knocked down again.

Barnby listens to his father laughing. He sees the smile on his father's face, so wide, so bright, shining all the way to his eyes. Then Gather's tail sways his way again. He gets swept to the ground and, with his father, he laughs and laughs and laughs.

"Gather! Gather, we found you!" Mrs. Simson shouts above the laughing and the crowd.

The sound of Mrs. Simson's voice reaches Gather's ears. The great sloth stops and slowly turns around. She brings her big head right down to Mrs. Simson and gives her a sniff.

"Hello, my friend," says Mrs. Simson, stroking the fur on Gather's prehistoric cheek. "It's good to see you again."

But Gather is hungry. She twists back around and starts moving again in the direction of her supper.

"Where's she going?" Hi asks.

"Anywhere she wants," says Barnby. Angel thinks that's the funniest answer ever.

Officer Grant moves to the front of the sloth to keep the way clear and to walk next to Jomon.

"Are you taking me back to jail?" he asks.

"Yes."

"You can't have him yet," says Hi. "He has something he has to do first."

To get to the forest and the cannonball trees, Gather follows the road through the village. It is not a smooth walk. There are cars and bicycles, minivans and carts pulled by horses. There are mounds of melons, bright umbrellas over stands of plantain chips and colorful displays of dresses.

And there are people going about their ordinary day in their ordinary way — some with smiles, some with scowls, some looking tired and some so deep in their own thoughts that they barely see what's around them.

Then they see Gather, and everything changes.

The frazzled mother about to yell at her kids sees Gather and holds her children gently out of the way. Two men in an argument about who owes who and how much, see Gather and the debt is forgotten.

No one shouts. No one is afraid.

The crowd behind Gather grows and sticks with her as she leaves the road and heads across a field that will bring her closer to the forest and food.

Jomon hears Mrs. Simson answering questions from the crowd.

"She won't bite you," says Mrs. Simson. "She only eats plants. You're right, we don't see many like her around anymore."

Between the field and the trees is a cemetery. Gather walks straight through the rows of grave markers to a cannonball tree. To the oohs and aahs of the crowd, she raises herself up on her haunches until she is taller than most of the buildings in Guyana. She reaches out an arm, plucks a stalk of flowers with her long, curved fingernails, and begins to eat.

Everyone watches.

Jomon stands ten feet away in a line with Hi, Angel, Barnby and Officer Grant. People fill in behind them and around them, giving Gather plenty of space to enjoy her meal.

Jomon watches people take selfies with Gather, but from a respectful distance, not trying to pet her or interfere with her. He sees a camera crew arrive from a television station.

He sees tiny blue flowers, yellow butterflies and a procession of leaf-cutter ants crossing a fallen tree. He sees old people showing things to young people, and children pointing to a woodpecker high in a tonka tree.

All around him, people are pulling up weeds and tidying long-neglected graves. He sees people pushing others in wheelchairs, residents of the local care home, so that they can be part of the event, too. He hears some people praying, some people singing, and some people saying, "Here's your great-aunt Ada's grave. Did I tell you about her? She was always so nice to me. Eyes in the back of her head, though. I couldn't get away with a thing!"

"What now?" he asks Officer Grant.

"I'm guessing Gather will make her way into the forest and go deeper and deeper into the heart of Guyana."

"You're not going to kill her and put her back in the museum?"

"Oh, no. My job is to find runaways and make sure they end up in a good home." Officer Grant smiles. "Today, for Gather, my job is done."

"Your mother is buried right through there," says Barnby, nodding to a path through the trees.

Jomon looks at Officer Grant.

"Jomon," she says, "the jail is not going anywhere. Go find your mother."

32

Jomon walks out of the sunshine and into a shady grove. The trees here hold each other's branches like they're holding hands. The branches form an arched ceiling, like in a cathedral. A flock of red macaws look like Christmas ornaments against the deep green leaves.

Jomon steps quietly around the graves, looking at the names carved into the stones.

He finds Taylor, his mother's last name before she was married.

Then, at the end of the row, he finds his mother.

Corrine Anne Taylor (Fowler)
Mother of Jomon
She let her light shine.

Jomon kneels by the grave. He pulls the weeds away from the headstone and traces the carved letters of her name with the tip of his finger.

"Hi, Mum," he whispers. "It's me."

He runs his fingers through the grass.

"I'm sorry it took so long for me to get here," he says, "but I'm here now. And I'll be back again. It might be a while …"

He can't tell his mum he's going to jail.

Should he sing or pray or make a speech?

Jomon doesn't want to do any of those things. He wants to stay on the grass, close by her name, and just sit.

She's in a nice quiet spot, he thinks.

The grove is cool. Jomon looks around the calm beauty of the place, then blinks and looks again.

He is sitting in Jomonland. There is even a stream gurgling along the edge. All that's missing is the bench.

Maybe I can build one, he thinks, then says, "I'll be back with a bench."

He takes Cora's tissue-paper flower out of his pocket and places it on his mum's grave.

"See you soon, Mum," he says. Then he gets up and leaves the grove.

Officer Grant is waiting.

"I'm ready to go back to the detention center now," he says.

"And I'm ready to take you. But we have one stop to make first."

She turns Jomon around so that he is facing her, and looks him in the eye.

"Jomon," she says, "we found your father. He's alive."

33

Jomon is asleep on his bed, in his school uniform and his stocking feet.

It is the middle of the night.

He wakes up thirsty.

He gets out of bed, walks past the tiny bathroom and into the combined sitting room and kitchen. There's more room for sitting since his father sold the fridge and stove for booze, but there's no point in sitting there since the television has also been turned into booze. Even if the television was still there, the electric bill hasn't been paid.

Jomon rinses out a tea mug. He wonders sleepily how long before the landlord finds out his father sold the appliances, and whether that will mean police and eviction or just eviction.

He fills the mug with water, then turns around to lean against the sink while he drinks it.

The mug hits the floor with no water reaching his lips.

Jomon's father is sprawled on the sofa. His face droops to the side, eyes closed, mouth open. Empty bottles lie scattered on the floor.

The light from the street allows Jomon to see his father's chest. It is not moving.

His father is not breathing.

Jomon bolts from the house and out into the dark, lonely night.

The door slams behind him.

He just keeps running.

34

"Here's what we think happened."

Officer Grant is standing by the open back door of the police car, leaning in and talking to Jomon. Behind her are Hi, Angel, Barnby and Mrs. Simson. They are in the parking lot of the Georgetown Public Hospital.

"We talked with a neighbor who heard the door slam. We think the noise woke your father just long enough for him to get out of the house and run after you. He collapsed again a few blocks away. He had no identification and no one in the area knew him, so we didn't know who he was until the old woman next door went into the hospital to visit someone else and saw him in a bed on the ward."

"He's really alive?" asks Angel.

"He's in a coma from the combination of pills and alcohol."

"Will he be all right?" Barnby asks.

"I don't know," says Officer Grant. "Jomon, get out of the car. I'll take you to him."

"I don't want to see him."

"I do," says Barnby. "We'll all go."

All the other doors of the car are closed and locked. There is only one way out for Jomon.

He swings his feet out of the car. Officer Grant leads the way. Mrs. Simson brings up the rear.

"He's on the third floor," Officer Grant says.

Each step is a mountain.

Jomon climbs and he thinks.

He thinks about his mum, and about the bench he's going to build and put beside her grave.

He thinks about little Cora, who gave him a flower.

He thinks about Gather, a creature impossible that he saw with his own eyes.

He thinks about everything that has happened since the geography competition, and he thinks about the time he is going to have to do in youth jail.

When he gets to the door of the third-floor ward, all he has are thoughts. No answers.

"He's down this way," says Officer Grant quietly.

They move through the ward, past patients in casts,

patients with tubes, patients with visitors and patients alone.

Jomon's father is alone.

Jomon stops when he sees him.

"You can do this," whispers Hi.

His father looks like he's sleeping. He is clean, in a clean bed, and the smells are of antiseptic and good cooking coming up from the kitchen.

There is a chair by the bed. Jomon sits down, and he takes his father's hand.

This is the hand that held a bottle and formed a fist.

This is also the hand that held young Jomon's tiny one and got him safely across the street to the park.

The grandfathers stand together at the end of his bed.

I can end this, Jomon thinks. *I can be the first one to be … happy.*

In that moment, Jomon decides to try.

"I'm going to live," he says out loud.

The grandfathers smile and nod.

Then, in front of Jomon's eyes, they age. They transform into the old, old men they would have grown into if they hadn't killed themselves. They all have wrinkles and gray hair. They all have smiles that reach all the way to their eyes.

They begin to fade, and then they are gone.

Jomon squeezes his father's hand.

He, Jomon will live. That is his decision. He may need to make this decision again and again. Life is hard and it is not going to get easier. But he feels ready for it. After all, he has a lot of people backing him up.

Jomon looks into his father's face.

Then he does what the men in his family have always done, down through the generations, when someone they love is hurting.

He sings the Soothing Song.

—

The End

AUTHOR'S NOTE

Dear Reader,

Many people around the world and throughout history have struggled as Jomon does in this story. Life can be hard. We can feel alone. We can feel that our present pain will be forever pain.

It can be difficult to remember that things change and that we change in our ability to deal with them. We need to find a way to hang on through the tough times and trust in our ability to create a better life for ourselves.

Thank you for sharing Jomon's journey with me. May your own journey be full of good work, enduring wonder and broad horizons.

All the best,

Deborah Ellis

If you or someone you know is in crisis, please contact one of these organizations:

- National Suicide Prevention Lifeline (a network of local crisis centers that provide free and confidential emotional support to people in suicidal crisis or emotional distress, 24 hours a day, 7 days a week)
  suicidepreventionlifeline.org
  1-800-273-TALK (8255)

- The LifeLine Canada Foundation (TLC promotes positive mental health and suicide prevention/awareness)
  thelifelinecanada.ca
  1-833-456-4566

- Kids Help Phone (Canada's only 24/7 national service offering professional counseling, referrals and volunteer-led, text-based support for young people in English and French)
  kidshelpphone.ca
  1-800-668-6868

- The Trevor Project — Saving Young LGBTQ Lives (a national 24-hour, toll-free confidential suicide hotline for LGBTQ youth)
  thetrevorproject.org
  1-866-488-7386

ACKNOWLEDGMENTS

I would like to express my deep appreciation to the people of Guyana I met on my visit there with Mental Health Without Borders. And a big thank you to Shelley Tanaka who, as always, helped me find the story through the fog.

— Deborah Ellis

The author and publisher are grateful for the input of Dr. Rachel Ptashny and other mental-health professionals who read and commented on the manuscript. We have also taken into account the guidelines recommended by the National Action Alliance for Suicide Prevention. theactionalliance.org

DEBORAH ELLIS is a Member of the Order of Canada. She has won the Governor General's Award, the University of California's Middle East Book Award, Sweden's Peter Pan Prize and the Jane Addams Children's Book Award. She is best known for her Breadwinner series, which has been published in twenty-five languages, with $2 million in royalties donated to Canadian Women for Women in Afghanistan and Street Kids International. Deborah lives in Simcoe, Ontario. deborahellis.com